Dreamweaver Diaries Unlocked

A Pick•Your•Path•Adventure

Eric Johnson

Broken Table
Press

To Leo.

*Always remember,
the path you take in life
is yours to choose.*

Dreamweaver Diaries Unlocked

To Leo.

Always remember,
the path you take in life
is yours to choose.

Dreamweaver Diaries Unlocked

"Mom, I'm home, finally," you call out, shutting the front door behind you. The familiar, reassuring click of the lock engaging fills the air as you release your heavy bag to the ground, a resounding thud. The weight of your day seems to pull at your shoulders, but you've finally returned to the sanctuary of your home. With an exhausted sigh, you exhale all the stress that has built up throughout the long hours at school.

"How was school today?" Your mother's voice, sweet and full of concern, drifts from the kitchen, reaching your ears like a warm embrace.

"Long, and boring," you reply, your voice heavy with fatigue, though touched with a hint of resignation. The distant, soothing sounds of dishes clinking together in the kitchen make it evident that dinner has come and gone, and you've missed it. You can't help but feel a pang of regret for not being able to join your family and savor the simple pleasure of their company while you were locked in a battle with that never-ending English project.

As you stand in the entrance hall, pondering your next move, two options present themselves like diverging paths in a forest. The inviting aroma wafting from the kitchen and your mother's presence beckon you to go talk to her. A conversation, a comforting hug, and a warm meal await, a source of solace and support to ease your burdens.

On the other hand, the allure of your room, the private sanctuary where you can escape from the world and unwind, is equally enticing. Upstairs, you can retreat into the comforting embrace of solitude, perhaps immersing yourself in a good book, your favorite music, or simply lying down to find solace in the quietude.

The choice is yours to make. Do you follow the siren's call of the kitchen, where love and a warm meal reside, or do you ascend the stairs to your room, where the solace of solitude awaits to soothe your tired soul?

- <u>Talk to your mother in the kitchen.</u> (Page 3)

- <u>Go upstairs to your room.</u> (Page 5)

You walk into the warmly lit kitchen, the soft, golden glow of the overhead light enveloping you like a comforting hug. With a sense of contentment, you plop down at the kitchen table. The room is filled with the delicious aroma of beef stew, the hearty scent of simmered meat, tender vegetables, and freshly baked bread, making your stomach grumble with anticipation.

Your mother, a culinary magician in her own right, is tidying up and carefully putting away the leftovers. She turns to you with a loving smile, her eyes crinkling at the corners, a testament to years of shared laughter and memories.

"I'm just packing up the leftovers, do you want any?" she asks, her voice full of warmth and affection.

"Please," you say enthusiastically, your mouth already watering. "I love your beef stew."

With practiced grace, she retrieves a large bowl from the cupboard and ladles a generous serving of the fragrant stew into it. The savory scent of the potatoes and thick, rich broth swirls around you, making your stomach grumble even louder in eager anticipation.

She places the steaming bowl in front of you, and you can't help but offer a grateful smile. The sight of the hearty meal fills you with a sense of comfort, a reminder that in this place, your mother's love and care are unconditional.

Your mother leaves you at the table and returns to the task of packing the leftovers. The kitchen seems to come alive around you as you sit there, the clinking of dishes and the occasional sound of the refrigerator door punctuating the tranquility. You're faced with two choices: One option is to engage your mother in conversation, to talk about your day, to share your triumphs and challenges. The other is to enjoy the comforting warmth of the kitchen and your mother's presence in quiet companionship, savoring every spoonful of her delicious beef stew, the food that nourishes not only your body but also your soul.

The choice is yours to make. Do you engage in conversation, or do you savor the stew in quiet, loving companionship?

- ◉ <u>Talk about your day.</u> (Page 8)
- ◉ <u>Eat quietly.</u> (Page 11)

"I'm going to head upstairs to get my homework done," you say, shouldering your backpack that you retrieved from the front hall, and then you head to your bedroom.

"Alright, hun," your mother calls after you, her voice tinged with a hint of concern. "Just don't stay up too late doing homework; sleep is important, you know."

"Okay, Mom," you reply, heading upstairs with a smile that humors her request, even though you're well aware that it's a promise you might not keep. With all this homework piling up, you're beginning to doubt if you'll ever get to bed at a reasonable hour.

Sitting down at the desk in your room, you open your laptop and start doing the research that your group members were supposed to have done already. This is precisely why you don't like working in groups.

As you dig into the work, a deep frustration builds within you. It's not fair that you're stuck here working while your group members are probably out having fun or getting a good night's sleep. The fatigue creeps up on you, and you feel sleep pulling at your eyelids, urging them to close. But you fight to keep them open, reminding yourself of the looming deadline and the importance of completing the assignment.

However, exhaustion wins the battle, and your head starts to droop. Your surroundings blur, and then, suddenly, you find yourself in the middle of a dark, mysterious forest. The towering trees block out most of the moon's faint light, casting eerie shadows across the forest floor.

"Hello?" you call into the gathering fog, but there's no response. The silence is oppressive, even the normal sounds of the wilderness absent.

Driven by a sense of unease, you begin to walk through the woods. There's no discernible path, so you weave your way among the trees, making your way toward a distant, flickering campfire that pierces the darkness. As you draw nearer, the flames come into focus, but the overwhelming silence remains.

Approaching the clearing around the campfire, you see several people you vaguely recognize. They appear to be engaged in a heated conversation, their expressions intense and animated. Yet, the eerie silence persists.

"Hello," you say again, raising your voice to get their attention, "can you hear me?"

Despite your efforts, the people around the campfire remain oblivious to your presence. Their pantomime continues, growing more frantic by the moment. It's as if they're in the midst of a terrible argument, but you can't make out a single word.

Then, in an instant, they all rise as one and back away from the fire, their terrified expressions now directed at something behind you. You turn to face the darkness and peer into the depths of the forest, but you can't see what's causing their panic.

As your heart races and the adrenaline courses through your veins, you finally spot it. Looming over the campfire, a creature materializes from mist and shadow. Its elongated, clawed fingers gleam ominously in the moonlight, and you're overwhelmed by feelings of anger and devastation.

- <u>Greet the creature.</u> (Page 16)

- <u>Attack the creature.</u> (Page 18)

- <u>Cower in fear.</u> (Page 20)

As you savor the savory stew, the comforting flavors fill your mouth, making you forget the troubles of the day for a moment. It's as if every bite warms not only your belly but also your soul.

"You would not believe the horrible day I had today," you finally confide, once the initial hunger has been satisfied.

"Oh no," your mother says, her expression a mix of concern and empathy. She puts the leftovers in the fridge and joins you at the table. "What happened?"

Over the course of the meal, you recount the series of frustrating events that made your day miserable. The combination of the warm, homemade food and the cathartic experience of sharing your woes with your mother begins to lighten your heart. By the time you finish your stew, you feel much better than you did when you first arrived home.

With a sense of contentment and gratitude, you help your mother with the dishes. You both work together in companionable silence, a gesture of shared love and understanding.

"I'm going to head upstairs to get my homework done," you say, slinging your backpack over your shoulder and heading for the front hall, then upstairs to your bedroom.

"Alright, hun," your mother calls after you. "Just don't stay up too late doing homework; sleep is important, you know."

"Okay, Mom," you reply, giving a little smile, as if to assure her that you'll heed her advice, even though your impending workload suggests otherwise. With all this homework hanging over your head, the idea of getting to bed at a reasonable hour feels like a distant dream.

Yet, after sharing your day and problems with your mother, you realize that things aren't as insurmountable as they seemed. Sometimes, just talking about your struggles makes them feel more manageable.

You work diligently on your homework for a while, but eventually, the lure of your comfortable bed becomes irresistible. You recall that you'll have some time during your study period tomorrow, and you can always discuss your predicament with your teacher, given that your partners didn't hold up their end of the project. With this in mind, the importance of sleep becomes evident.

You gather your school materials, pack your bag for the next day, and head for your bed, curling up beneath the soft, warm covers. The weight of the day gradually fades as you drift into a peaceful sleep.

And then, you find yourself in a beautiful, well-lit field. The golden sun shines brightly on your back as you recline beside a serene pond. Nature unfolds before you – a pair of graceful deer prance across the field, and a fluffy bunny hops to the water's edge to take a delicate drink.

At the edge of this idyllic field, you spot a dense, enigmatic forest, its darkness in stark contrast to the brightness of the field. The peace of the field beckons, offering a serene respite, while the forest holds the allure of adventure.

- <u>**Stay in the well-lit field.**</u> (Page 23)

- <u>**Explore the forest.**</u> (Page 25)

As you savor each spoonful of your mother's delicious beef stew, the rich flavors dance on your taste buds, offering solace after a long and tiresome day. The warmth of the thick broth permeates your being, and the hearty potatoes and tender chunks of beef fill your stomach, bringing both comfort and sustenance.

Having basked in the nurturing embrace of your mother's cooking, you lean back in your chair, your body slowly absorbing the nourishment. The aroma of the freshly baked bread still lingers in the air, enveloping you in a cozy ambiance. For a moment, you forget about the frustrations and weariness that had weighed you down upon your return.

However, the looming burden of an unfinished project and the realization that your group members haven't been as responsible as you'd hoped soon resurface. The sense of injustice and the pressure to excel wrestle with the soothing effects of the meal, causing an inner turmoil.

You finally decide to act on your academic responsibilities. "I'm going to head upstairs to get my homework done," you declare, pushing your chair back as you rise from the table. You fetch your backpack from the front hall and make your way to your bedroom.

Your mother's voice trails after you, her concern evident as she calls out, "Just don't stay up too late doing homework, sleep is important, you know."

With a nod, you respond, "Okay, Mom," as you continue up the stairs, intending to humor her with the promise of a reasonable bedtime. Yet, the mountain of homework ahead makes you doubt whether that promise can be fulfilled.

Upon reaching your room, you settle at your desk, illuminated by the soft glow of your laptop screen. You open it and begin delving into the research, a task that was supposed to have been completed by your group members. The frustration grows as you realize that you're left to pick up the slack in a group project, a common source of vexation for diligent students like yourself.

As you sit at your desk, frustration festers within you. The unfairness of your group project gnaws at your thoughts like an itch you can't scratch. You're convinced that your fellow group members are either having more fun than you are or enjoying a peaceful slumber while you're toiling away. The weight of the tasks you've taken on and the looming deadlines seem almost insurmountable.

You continue to work, your eyes locked onto the laptop screen, but sleep's siren call grows ever stronger. Fatigue tugs at your eyelids, and your head starts to droop under the crushing weight of exhaustion. With a heroic effort, you attempt to fight off the encroaching drowsiness, determined to complete your research. However, the struggle proves futile, and you gradually surrender to the irresistible lure of sleep.

As you close your eyes, an abyss of darkness swallows you, replacing the familiar contours of your room with a surreal, dreamlike landscape. You find yourself in the midst of a dark forest, where towering trees reach for the sky, their branches intertwined to blot out the moon's feeble light.

"Hello?" you call out into the thick, oppressive fog, but only silence responds. The usual sounds of scurrying woodland creatures or the gentle hum of insects are conspicuously absent. The unnaturally heavy silence hangs in the air, observed even by the rustling leaves above.

Despite the lack of a discernible path, you start to navigate the tangled woods. Each step becomes a venture into the unknown, guiding you toward a distant campfire that flickers like a beacon. The closer you get, the more palpable the silence becomes, oppressive and all-encompassing.

As you finally break through the tree line into the clearing surrounding the campfire, a group of individuals, vaguely familiar to you, engage in a conversation you cannot hear. Their animated gestures and pantomime grow more agitated as you stand among them. You attempt to address them, to bridge the divide between their world and yours.

"Hello," you say once more, a hopeful attempt to capture their attention. "Can you hear me?"

However, the individuals gathered around the campfire remain unresponsive. Their collective panic becomes evident as they rise from their places, retreating towards you. Their terrified expressions and frantic movements tell you that something ominous lurks in the shadows of the forest behind them.

Turning your attention away from the fleeing campers, you finally see the source of their terror. Looming over the fire, a creature takes shape, seemingly forged from mist and shadow. It defies understanding, and its very presence radiates malevolence. Long, claw-like fingers extend from its form, each one emitting an eerie, dark glow under the waxing moon.

Feelings of anger and devastation churn within you, but adrenaline courses through your veins, ready to drive your decision.

- ◉ <u>Speak to the creature.</u> (Page 16)

- ◉ <u>Attack the creature.</u> (Page 27)

- ◉ <u>Cower in fear.</u> (Page 20)

As you gazed up at the towering, shadowy figure before you, a shiver of intimidation coursed through your entire being. The presence of this enigmatic entity exuded an overwhelming sense of sadness and desperation, as though it were suffering under some weighty burden. Despite its eerie appearance, a strange empathy welled up within you, compelling you to offer assistance to this unfortunate creature.

"Can I help you?" you inquired, your voice trembling only slightly, as you sought to mask the underlying panic. The darkness that shrouded the figure seemed to undulate and swirl in the night breeze, and your innate compassion pushed you to extend a helping hand.

The shadow responded with a voice that resonated through the clearing, echoing with a sense of strength and authority. "Why have you come here?" it questioned, its words carrying a weighty significance.

In response, you hesitated, realizing that you were uncertain of your own intentions in this unfamiliar and surreal forest. "You know," you confessed, your voice wavering, "just passing through."

The shadow, however, was unmoved by your response, standing resolutely in your path. "Then pass through," it declared, its form still blocking your way. "But know that down the road a bit there is an abandoned cottage, and in that cottage is my next victim. You, you are a nuance that I will deal with if I have to, but you are not worth my time. You are not my target."

- <u>Walk through the Shadow.</u> (Page 31)
- <u>This ends now!</u> (Page 33)

As you faced the shadowy entity, an overwhelming surge of bravery coupled with a touch of recklessness welled up within you. You squared your shoulders, preparing to confront this mysterious adversary head-on. With a deep breath, you dropped into a fighting stance, bending your knees and clenching your fists, just as you'd seen countless heroes do in television shows. You were convinced you were the hero in this story, and that confidence fueled your resolve to emerge victorious.

The palpable emotions of fear and desperation radiating from the shadow threatened to rattle your nerve, but you steeled yourself, determined to make this confrontation count. With a burst of determination, you launched yourself at the looming figure, aiming to knock it off balance and gain the upper hand in this sudden brawl. However, instead of connecting with a solid form, you passed right through the shadow, landing hard on the ground with the wind knocked out of you.

Realizing your mistake, you clambered to your feet, the urgency of the situation pushing you to your limits. With adrenaline coursing through your veins, you set off running through the forest, your heart pounding in your chest. The branches clawed at your clothing, and the mournful howl of the shadow lingered ominously in the air behind you, growing steadily closer.

In your haste, you arrived at a fork in the path, flanked by thick undergrowth, and you knew you had a critical decision to make.

- <u>Take the path to the left.</u> (Page 35)
- <u>Take the path to the right.</u> (Page 36)
- <u>Hide in the undergrowth.</u> (Page 44)
- <u>Turn and fight the Shadow.</u> (Page 33)

The air hung heavy with a chilling silence, interrupted only by the diminishing sound of the campers' frantic footsteps and the quiet crackle of the dying fire. In the wake of their departure, a feeling of dread settled over the clearing like dew on morning grass. Their panic was infectious, and as it seeped into my bones, I was frozen, caught between an instinctual need to flee and a paralyzing terror.

I could feel the campers' fear still lingering, a psychological residue that clung to my thoughts, making my skin crawl. It wasn't just the sight of their wide, terrified eyes or the way their breaths hissed through clenched teeth. It was in the way they moved—uncoordinated yet desperately fast, like deer bounding away from a forest fire. A twig snapped loudly under my own heel, a discordant note in the otherwise muted forest, and I winced, my heart rate spiking.

The girl with the ponytail had left me with a silent scream trapped in her gaze, a look that told me more than words ever could. Yet here I stood, rooted to the spot as if the ground had grown hands and gripped my ankles tight. That's when the breeze brushed against my face, a harbinger of something sinister. It carried an odor that was at once sweet and putrid, a scent that the part of your brain that's still animal recognized as dangerous.

My breath hitched as I sensed it—the presence of the creature that had spurred the campers into their maddened dash.

The cold fear that had whispered through me turned into a scream, echoing in my veins, urging me to make a choice. I turned slowly, the world tilting on its axis as I came face-to-face with the unknown.

The creature was a nightmare made manifest. The fire, once robust and alive with dancing flames, was now a bed of glowing embers as the creature hovered over it. The darkness it brought was oppressive, pressing against my eyes, trying to seep into my mind. It moved with a fluid grace that belied its monstrous form, tendrils of shadow and smoke weaving together to create a shape that my eyes could barely comprehend. Its form seemed to shift and change, a puzzle that the mind couldn't solve, flickering at the edges as if it were barely contained by this reality.

Silent as a grave, it drifted, and the air grew colder, the remaining light from the embers reflecting off what might have been eyes—deep, endless pits that threatened to swallow me whole. The darkness seemed to stretch towards me, a question posed in the space between us. Was it curiosity or malice that propelled it? I couldn't tell.

In that moment, a choice presented itself, stark as the creature against the night: Stand still and hope, like the campers, it doesn't see you. Merge with the shadows and become another silent witness to this eerie spectacle, another trembling form in the darkness, banking on the slim chance that it would pass by untouched.

Or, follow the campers. Allow your feet to reclaim their purpose, to turn and bolt into the labyrinth of trees, to stumble through underbrush and over roots, to push through the fear that says you may not be fast enough, that your breaths could become ragged gasps like theirs, that your own eyes could hold that silent scream when you glance back for just a moment.

With the creature so close, its darkness caressing the edge of my consciousness, the decision hung in the air, heavy and significant, like the choice between waking and forever succumbing to a nightmare.

- ◉ <u>Stand still and hope it doesn't see you.</u> (Page 46)
- ◉ <u>Follow the campers.</u> (Page 44)

Under the gentle caress of the morning light, your eyes fluttered open. The serenity of your dreams lingered, a soothing balm to the rush of waking life. Throughout the night, you had journeyed through dreams so vivid and gentle that reality seemed to embrace you just as warmly upon your return. In your slumber, there was no chaos, only the tranquil whisper of imaginary streams and the tender rustling of leaves that orchestrated a symphony of peace. The world within your mind had been a sanctuary, an idyllic realm where the soul could dance, unburdened and pure.

As you rose, the refreshing clarity that only comes from a night of profound rest filled you. Your limbs moved with ease, each step buoyed by the restfulness of your sojourn through the land of dreams. The day ahead seemed less daunting, colored by the afterglow of your nocturnal escapades. Yet, for all the quiet joy your dreams had bestowed, you sensed that the deeper magic —the craft of the Dreamweaver—remained elusive.

Your dreams, though beautiful, had been yours alone to wander, not to weave. The realization was clear and without sorrow. Not every dreamer is a Dreamweaver, at least, not without the knowledge of how to harness the hidden threads of the night.

You did not become a Dreamweaver this time, but with every night comes another possibility.

The End

The darkness of the forest presses in on you, thick as a shroud. Ancient trees stand as silent sentinels, their gnarled limbs ensnaring the scant moonlight, fracturing it into silver slithers that barely touch the ground. The fog weaves through their trunks, a creeping tide that swallows sound and chokes the night with its opalescent embrace.

"Hello?" Your voice emerges as a frail trespasser in this mute world, swallowed whole by the fog. No echo returns to you, only the oppressive weight of a silence so complete it drowns out the beat of your own heart. Not a cricket's chirp nor the whisper of nocturnal hunters reaches your ears. The very air feels stagnant, reluctant to carry any disturbance through its dense, misty body.

Each step you take toward the distant glimmer of the campfire is a study in mounting dread. Your feet move soundlessly across a carpet of fallen leaves and pine needles, as if the forest itself mutes your passage, complicit in the night's eerie stillness.

The campfire grows larger, its flames a ballet of orange and red, yet it casts no welcoming warmth. The faces of the people you recognize are pale and drawn, their mouths moving in silent discourse, their gestures sharp with urgency. You call out, a plea for some acknowledgment, but they remain oblivious, enclosed in a bubble of silence.

Their sudden movement, a collective shudder, has them stumbling back towards you, eyes wide with an unnamed terror. As they flee, the silence fractures, giving way to the distant, desperate sounds of their flight—branches snapping, leaves crunching underfoot—fading quickly into nothingness.

Alone, you turn. The snapping twig behind you is the prelude to horror made manifest. The creature—it defies nature's design, a specter formed from the darkness itself, a gaping maw of emptiness where a face might be, and fingers ending in claws that promise pain and obliteration. It stands as if a king over its domain, the once vibrant campfire dying to a feeble flicker in its presence.

A palpable aura of malice emanates from it, a force so potent it feels like a physical blow. Your heart races, pumping fear and adrenaline in equal measure through your veins. In the dim light, you see it more clearly—the ethereal monster of your darkest nightmares, its presence an abomination against the living world.

Now, the forest holds its breath with you. Time stretches, a thin thread about to snap. You are at the precipice, a decision clawing its way to the forefront.

- <u>Speak to the creature.</u> (Page 16)

- <u>Attack the creature.</u> (Page 27)

- <u>Cower in fear.</u> (Page 20)

As you stand your ground, the atmosphere crackles with the impending clash. You are the lone bulwark against the consuming darkness, a solitary figure of defiance amidst the whispering trees. The shadow looms over you, a colossus carved from the night itself, its form undulating with sinister intent.

You summon every ounce of bravery – or perhaps it's folly – as you steel yourself for combat. Your stance is that of a pugilist from the tales of old, knees slightly bent, fists clenched with a resolve that belies your inexperience. In your mind's eye, you're the stalwart hero of countless small-screen epics, poised to triumph against the impossible.

Despite your resolve, the air around you grows colder, the darkness denser. You can feel it – the sorrow and despair that this entity exudes like a miasma, a tangible force seeking to cripple your spirit. Yet, you stand firm, the fire of determination in your gaze unwavering.

With a battle cry torn from the depths of your being, you launch yourself at the shadow, aiming to disrupt its form with sheer physicality. In those fleeting seconds, your heart races with the thrill of the hero's charge, the desperate gamble for victory.

But as you collide with the shadow, the world shifts. You're met not with the resistance of flesh or the solidity of substance but with the cold embrace of the void. Your momentum carries you through the ephemeral mass, and you emerge to the unforgiving reality of the forest floor.

The air is knocked from your lungs in a violent rush, the ground punishing you for your audacity. Disoriented and gasping for breath, you scramble to your feet, the taste of loam and defeat bitter on your tongue. The shadow hasn't moved, and for a heart-stopping moment, it feels as though it watches you – a silent, oppressive judge.

You know now the futility of physical combat against this spectral adversary. With lungs still heaving, you pivot on a heel and sprint into the forest's embrace, following the wake of the campers' flight. Branches lash out like grasping fingers, and roots rise up to catch unsuspecting feet, but you do not slow. Panic and adrenaline become your fuel, propelling you through the darkness.

Somewhere behind, the presence of the shadow looms, a reminder of the dread that spurred your flight. The forest seems to close in around you, and the line between hunter and hunted blurs. You cannot fight the shadow with fists and fury, but perhaps there is another way to bring an end to this nightmare.

And so you run, the terror at your back and an uncertain hope before you.

- <u>Run from the Shadow.</u> (Page 29)

The world around you has narrowed to the rapid pounding of your heart and the ragged draw of breath that burns in your chest. The trees whip past in a blur, each one an indistinct figure in the sea of darkness that envelopes the forest. The thorns and wayward branches snatch at your clothing with grasping fingers, leaving behind small rips and the sting of scratches on your skin.

Behind you, the mournful howl of the shadow fills the night, a sorrowful lament that chills your blood and propels you forward with even greater urgency. The sound seems to come from everywhere and nowhere, an omnipresent specter haunting your every step.

As you barrel through the forest, desperate to escape the clutches of this nightmare, the path before you splits into two, diverging into separate veins that penetrate deeper into the heart of the woods. To the right, the path is narrow, hemmed in by towering trees that seem to lean inwards, their branches interlocking like the arches of a cathedral. To the left, the way is broader, but the underbrush grows wild and untamed, suggesting the path is less traveled and possibly hiding unforeseen dangers.

Thick undergrowth encroaches upon the clearing at the fork, dense and impenetrable, offering a potential hiding place but also the risk of becoming trapped, a sitting duck for the malevolent force that stalks you.

And then, there's the choice to no longer flee but to confront the encroaching terror. The shadow, a relentless pursuer, has driven you to this precipice of decision. Could there be a way to turn and fight, to face the darkness with an inner light you've yet to muster?

The shadow's howl crescendoes, a dirge for the damned that seems to be closing in with every passing second. It's a reminder that time is a luxury you do not possess.

- <u>Take the path to the left.</u> (Page 35)

- <u>Take the path to the right.</u> (Page 36)

- <u>Hide in the undergrowth.</u> (Page 44)

- <u>Turn and fight the Shadow.</u> (Page 33)

The moment of decision weighs heavy upon you, a suffocating blanket of dread and anticipation. The shadow looms, a sentinel of despair, its very presence a chilling testament to the night's eerie call. It is a barrier of darkness, a threshold between the known and the unfathomable. You pause, the impulse to turn back or flee to the sides gripping you, yet something inexplicable urges you forward—toward the shadow, toward the abandoned house that lies beyond.

With a fortitude that surprises even you, you advance. Each step toward the shadow feels like wading through a quagmire of fear, the air growing denser, the darkness deepening until it's as if the night itself were alive, whispering secrets in a language of silence.

As you reach the intangible barrier the shadow casts, a coldness grips you, sudden and invasive. It seeps through your clothing, clawing at your flesh, leaving a sheen of clamminess upon your skin. The temperature drop is swift, a plunge into unseen icy waters that steals your breath away. A shiver racks your body, not just from the cold but from the alien emotions that come unbidden with the contact.

Rage, pure and unadulterated, floods your senses, a crimson tide of indignation that feels both intimately yours and utterly foreign. It's a rage that could tear worlds asunder, that could scream into the void and challenge the very stars. It fills you to the brim, a vessel of fury and despair, and you stumble forward, almost intoxicated by the power of the emotions that are not your own.

Then, just as suddenly as it came, the rage dissipates as you break through to the other side of the shadow. The relief is palpable, like emerging from a stifling room into the coolness of night, yet it is not the coolness of peace. The air is still thick with the musk of unease, and the sense of something lost lingers, a whisper on the wind that might be a lamentation or a warning.

The path ahead is clear now, the house in the distance an ominous silhouette against the lesser darkness of the forest. The path to the abandoned house is fraught with the unknown, and as you tread forward, the leaves beneath your feet seem to crunch louder, as though echoing the rapid beat of your heart.

What secrets lie within those derelict walls? What memories are etched into the decaying wood and the shattered panes of glass that stare out like vacant eyes? The house stands as a tombstone to forgotten stories, and as you draw nearer, you can't shake the feeling that the shadow's passage has marked you, that you carry with you now a piece of its essence, a shard of its eternal rage.

- <u>You find an abandoned house.</u> (Page 48)

The revelation washes over you like a cold wave, chilling and inevitable. The creature before you, a wraith birthed from the abyss of nightmares, radiates malevolence. It is the embodiment of evil, a miasma of darkness that seeks to extinguish the light of life wherever it may flicker. The air around it seems to warp, the atmosphere charged with a vile intent so potent it raises the fine hairs on your neck and arms. This being, this shadow, it's not just a predator; it's the apex of every fear, every wicked thought given form.

The silence of the forest, once merely eerie, now pulses with unsung threat, the quiet before the tempest's wrath. The shadow drifts closer, and with it, the line between reality and the dark recesses of the mind blurs. The trees stand as silent witnesses, their gnarled branches casting twisted shadows that mimic the arms of the creature reaching out towards you. Every instinct screams to flee, to escape this confrontation with the unknown. But deep within, a well of resolve begins to rise; you know flight is not an option.

The shadow is a harbinger, an omen of what's to come if left unchecked. Today, it hunts others, but tomorrow, it could be you who is prey. You understand with a grave certainty that this darkness will persist, follow, and haunt you, not just in the physical world but in the recesses of your very soul. The fight is not a choice but a necessity, a stand not just for your own life, but for all it may come to claim.

The creature's approach is unhurried, its confidence palpable as it moves with an unnatural grace, a ballet of despair. You feel the moment stretching, the seconds elongating as you teeter on the precipice of action. Do you steel yourself for battle against this unknown horror, dropping into a stance that, while possibly futile, signifies your unwillingness to go gentle into that good night? Or do you scour the environment for anything, any clue or tool that might give you an edge in the looming confrontation?

- <u>Examine your surroundings.</u> (Page 50)
- <u>Drop into a fighting stance.</u> (Page 52)

Panic tightens its grip around your chest as you veer left, the murkier of the two paths swallowing you whole. Here, the darkness seems alive, a velvet curtain woven with threads of unseen menace. The trees are like hunched figures, their branches grasping, turning the already treacherous path into a labyrinth of shadows and deception. Behind you, the wail of the shadow pursues, a symphony of dread that propels your flight.

Your breath comes in short, sharp bursts, fear and adrenaline pumping through your veins. You can't afford to slow down, not even for a heartbeat. The path ahead is a blur, and you trust your instincts more than your sight in this oppressive gloom. Then, in a cruel twist of fate, a gnarled root clutches at your foot. Momentum cruelly snatched away, you're sent sprawling into the suffocating embrace of the underbrush, your shoulder colliding with the unyielding trunk of a tree.

Gasping for air, a bitter taste of defeat in your mouth, you roll over. The nightmare looms ever closer, its form a tidal wave of despair. The claws, like shards of midnight, stretch toward you, threatening to snuff out the light of your life. In a desperate, reflexive move, you raise your arms, your only shield against the coming onslaught. You squeeze your eyes shut begging for this to be just a dream.

⦿ <u>Continue</u> (Page 37)

As you veer onto the path to your right, the dense foliage seems to swallow you whole, its shadows stretching like fingers in the dim moonlight. Your footsteps, hurried and heavy, are the only sounds piercing the night's eerie stillness. The path, overgrown and barely discernible, winds through the oppressive thicket, a serpentine trail leading you deeper into uncertainty.

After what seems like an eternity of frantic running, the trees begin to thin, revealing a clearing. There, standing desolate and forlorn, is an old cottage. It stands like a relic of a bygone era, its structure weathered and worn, the paint peeling off in forlorn strips. The sight of it sends a shiver down your spine, not just because of its ghostly appearance, but because it represents your only chance at refuge. Its timeworn façade speaks of years neglected, windows like hollow eyes and a door slightly ajar, creaking softly in the night breeze. The building exudes a sense of abandonment and decay, but within its dilapidated walls lies the promise of a temporary refuge.

Your heart hammers in your chest, a relentless drumbeat of fear and exhaustion. You're out of breath, each inhale a labored gasp. The shadow, an ever-present threat, looms in your mind, its pursuit as inevitable as the night.

- <u>Hide in the cabin.</u> (Page 42)

- <u>Hide in the underbrush around the clearing.</u> (Page 44)

The pain is immediate and intense, like fire coursing through your veins. The shadow's claws, sharp as winter's chill, slice into you with an unnatural precision. As the searing heat spreads, it's chased by an icy numbness that creeps over your skin. It starts with your fingers, a sensation akin to being pricked by a thousand icy needles. The numbing cold slithers up your arms, turning your muscles to stone and leeching the strength from your bones.

You can't move, can't flee; you're a prisoner within your own flesh. The paralysis is ruthless, a creeping death that makes a mockery of your desperate yearning to survive. It encroaches upon your chest, and with it comes the suffocating realization that your breaths are numbered.

As the realization of your death comes, what are your final thoughts about?

- <u>Think about the loved ones you will miss.</u> (Page 38)

- <u>Think about the unfairness of life ending like this.</u> (Page 40)

Your chest aches with the weight of a thousand sunsets, each one a day spent in the warm embrace of family, the camaraderie of friends, the simple, pure moments that stitch the fabric of a life well-lived. Your mind's eye paints a mosaic of memories: the golden glow of candles on a birthday cake, the rippling laughter shared over holiday feasts, the spark of mischief in a friend's eye before a harmless prank. These memories are like lifelines, each a thread of color against the encroaching darkness.

Your eyes brim with tears, not just of sorrow, but of gratitude for the love you've known. The warmth of these recollections is a gentle balm, soothing the sting of your physical pain. The darkness may swallow your sight, but it cannot consume the light of the love you carry within.

The next sensation is the cool embrace of a gentle breeze and the soothing murmur of a babbling brook. You blink open your eyes to find yourself lying by the stream, the pain in your chest a fading echo, a distant memory that slips through your fingers like sand. Confusion clouds your mind; you can recall emotions, a sense of belonging, but the details elude you—names, faces, your very identity have all been washed away.

The sounds of convivial conversation beckon you, and instinctively, you are drawn toward the promise of company. As you approach, you sense that these people, these voices, hold the key to understanding your new existence.

In the dream world, you are reborn. Here, the life you once knew is but a distant dream itself. In this place, you will know the tranquil happiness of a world untethered by time or tragedy.

You have become a denizen of the dreamscape, an eternal resident in the tapestry of collective unconsciousness. Here, you will find solace, companionship, and an everlasting peace that the waking world could never offer.

As the sharp, biting pain recedes, a chilling realization dawns upon you — life's vibrant tapestry, once rich with the threads of future aspirations, love to be found, and triumphs to be savored, has been unceremoniously shredded. Your dreams, your hopes, your unwritten tomorrows, all snatched away by the capricious cruelty of the shadow. There's a bitter taste in your mouth, a silent scream at the injustice of it all. Your story was still being written, the ink not yet dry, and now the pages lie torn and scattered in the wind of fate.

In this merciless moment, a numbing cold spreads through your being, not the chill of the grave, but the frost of an existence unlived, of potential unfulfilled. As your consciousness wanes, there's a searing indignation that flares within the recesses of your soul, a bright, burning star of defiance against the night that seeks to consume you. Then, the darkness takes you, swallows you whole, an abyss from which there is no escape.

———————————

Now, you are adrift, disembodied yet bound by the very chains of emotion that marked your humanity. Fear grips you, not the fleeting terror of a nightmare, but a profound dread that seethes in the marrow of your spectral bones. Anger fuels your formless existence, a ferocious, untamed fury seeking an outlet, a target, an end to its ceaseless burning.

Despair, too, cloaks you like a shroud, a relentless tide that ebbs and flows with the memories of what you have lost, the life that was once yours to live. The emotions churn tumultuously within you, a storm with no eye, no calm, no quarter.

And so, you float, a specter fueled by a trifecta of torment, gliding silently through the slumbering world. In search of something to quench the inferno within, you become the very essence of fear, a shadow looming in the darkness of dreams.

You are the whisper in the night that quickens the heart, the presence that lingers in the corner of the eye, the dread that clutches at the souls of the sleeping. You are a monster, the embodiment of nightmares, the unseen terror that turns dreamscapes into realms of horror. You are the darkness that awaits in the silence, a fate once feared, now embraced.

The End

Stepping inside the cottage, a strange sense of comfort envelops you. The light softens, becoming warmer, more inviting. In the distance, you can hear the familiar sounds of your family, a balm to your frayed nerves. It feels like you've stepped into a safe haven, a sanctuary from the terror that lurks outside.

Suddenly, a knock at the door shatters the illusion of safety. Hesitant, you inch towards the sound, only to be greeted by the sight of a strange woman with a hawk perched on her shoulder. Fear grips you, and you retreat into the shadows of the room, your heart pounding with renewed intensity. Time drags on, and you're torn between the desire for rescue and the fear of the unknown.

Then, the distinct sound of a large bird and the rustling of feathers break the silence. A soft, reassuring voice follows, "It is safe, you can come out now, and we will get you home safely." Emerging from your hiding place, you're met by the sight of the woman, clad in casual attire but with an air of authority. The hawk on her shoulder regards you with an intelligence that seems almost human.

"Thank you so much," you manage to stammer out, overwhelmed by the surreal turn of events. She merely nods, guiding you to a door you hadn't noticed before. Walking through it, disorientation washes over you in waves.
Suddenly, you find yourself in the familiar surroundings of your bedroom, staring up at the ceiling. It feels like waking from a

standing like silent sentinels to your frantic escape. The moon, a pale witness in the sky, casts an eerie glow over the landscape, turning the familiar woods into a labyrinth of fear and uncertainty.

After what feels like an eternity of running, your eyes catch sight of salvation — a hollowed-out log from a fallen giant of the forest. The hole in its side promises a temporary refuge, a place to catch your breath and collect your thoughts. Without hesitation, you dive towards the log, your body fueled by pure survival instinct. You wiggle and squirm until you're safely inside, the rough bark scraping against your skin.

Crouched in the dark, cramped space, you try to quiet your heavy breathing, listening intently for any sign of the shadow. The sound of your heart pounding in your chest seems deafening in the silence of the log. Outside, the forest is eerily quiet, as if it too is holding its breath, waiting for what comes next.

The fear that grips you is visceral, a primal terror that gnaws at your mind. You're faced with a critical decision:

- <u>Keep hiding.</u> (Page 54)

- <u>Peek out to see the Shadow.</u> (Page 55)

- <u>Jump out and attack the Shadow.</u> (Page 33)

As the shadow looms ever closer, a tidal wave of emotions crashes over you, each one more intense and terrifying than the last. The air around you feels thick, charged with a malevolent energy that radiates from the shadow. It's as though the very essence of fear and despair has taken a physical form, advancing towards you with an inexorable, haunting pace.

Paralyzed by the overwhelming intensity of these emotions, you find yourself retreating step by step, your back scraping against the rough bark of a large tree. The tree stands as an unyielding barrier, its ancient trunk cold and unresponsive to

your plight. Your heart races, a frantic drumbeat in your chest, each thump echoing the terror that grips your very soul.

Sweat beads on your brow and your palms, the clamminess a stark contrast to the eerie chill of the night. Your breaths come in ragged, shallow gasps, as if the air itself is being stolen from your lungs by the approaching menace. The darkness of the forest seems to converge around the shadow, making it appear larger, more threatening, a specter of doom.

With your back against the tree and nowhere left to run, you slide down to the ground, your legs giving out under the weight of your fear. The ground beneath you is hard and unyielding, the fallen leaves and twigs offering no comfort. You are acutely aware of every sound, every movement of the shadow as it draws nearer.

- <u>Put your hands over your eyes and scream.</u> (Page 57)

- <u>Watch the Shadow approach.</u> (Page 37)

As you emerge into the clearing, the scene before you feels like something out of a forgotten story, a place lost to time and memory. The vine-covered trees encircle the space like silent guardians, their tendrils creeping over the branches and onto the ground, adding to the sense of abandonment.

The cottage, standing forlornly in the middle of the clearing, seems to sag with the weight of its own stories. What was once perhaps a happy, vibrant yellow now peels away in decaying strips, revealing the weathered wood beneath. The door, barely clinging to its final hinge, sways gently with each whisper of the wind, an eerie creaking sound that punctuates the silence.

Your swing is flawless, the kind of perfect, fluid motion that would indeed make any coach beam with pride. The branch connects with the Shadow, or rather, it passes through it. There is no resistance, no impact – just the eerie sensation of swinging through air, or perhaps through a wisp of smoke.

At that moment, a sound escapes the Shadow – a sigh, laden with centuries of sorrow, echoing with the weight of unspoken stories. The sigh seems to resonate in the very air around you, a mournful yet peaceful exhalation. As the branch completes its arc, the Shadow begins to dissipate, unraveling like mist in the dawn light.

Before your eyes, the terrifying form of the Shadow fragments, particles of darkness scattering into the night, leaving behind a stillness that is both eerie and serene. In the wake of its dissolution, you stand alone, the branch still clutched in your hands, under the gaze of the moon, a silent witness to the end of an ancient sorrow.

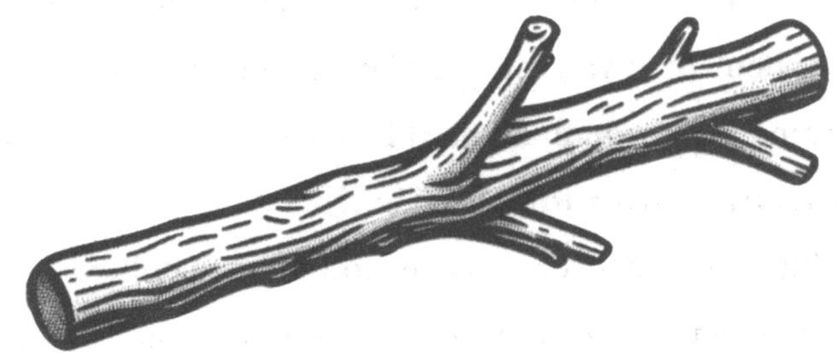

- <u>Continue</u> (Page 48)

As you settle into your fighting stance, a mixture of determination and trepidation pulses through you. Your knees are bent, your fists raised – a classic pose of readiness that feels somewhat out of place in the eerie, moonlit woods. Your experience in actual combat is limited to what you've seen in movies and TV shows, where the underdog hero triumphantly overcomes impossible odds. Drawing inspiration from these fictional battles, you try to embody that same heroism, hoping that confidence can somehow compensate for lack of training.

The Shadow moves toward you with an ethereal grace, its form billowing and shifting like smoke caught in a gentle breeze. It exudes an aura of fear and despair so tangible that it feels like a physical force pushing against you. You can almost see the waves of dark emotion rippling from its core, a visual representation of its tormented existence.

Despite the chilling aura that surrounds the Shadow, you steel your resolve. Your heart pounds in your chest, a drumbeat spurring you into action. With a shout that you hope sounds more confident than you feel, you launch yourself at the Shadow. In your mind's eye, you imagine this being the decisive moment, the valiant strike that turns the tide.

But reality shatters this illusion. As you collide with the Shadow, there's no impact, no sense of connection. Instead, you pass through it as if it were no more substantial than a wisp of fog. Your momentum unchecked, you crash to the forest floor, the breath knocked from your lungs in a painful whoosh. Leaves and twigs scrape against your skin as you tumble, a harsh reminder of the physical world you so desperately wish to defend.

Gasping for air, you manage to roll onto your back just in time to see the Shadow looming over you. Its claws, sharp and unyielding, descend with an inevitability that freezes your blood. In this moment, the stark reality of your situation becomes painfully clear: you're not in a TV show, and the Shadow is not an enemy that can be defeated with bravado and punches.

Lying there, defenseless, you're forced to confront not only the physical danger of the Shadow's claws but also the crushing realization of your own vulnerability. The stark contrast between your imagined heroism and your actual plight is a bitter pill to swallow as the Shadow's terrifying form eclipses the moonlight above you.

- <u>Search the ground around where you fell.</u> (Page 50)

- <u>Use your arms to fend off the Shadow's claws.</u> (Page 57)

Huddled in your hiding spot, you press yourself into the shadows, barely daring to breathe. The fear of being discovered by whatever malevolent force lurks outside is overwhelming. Your heart beats erratically, each thump echoing loudly in the confined space. The waiting is agonizing, time stretching out like a taut wire ready to snap. In an attempt to distract yourself, you rack your brain, trying to piece together the events that led you to this strange and perilous situation.

Emerging cautiously from your hiding place, you're greeted by an unexpected sight. A slender woman stands before you, dressed casually in jeans and a pink sweater adorned with a whimsical unicorn. But it's the thick leather covering her shoulders and the hawk perched upon her right shoulder that truly captivates your attention. The bird regards you with an intelligence that seems almost human, its eyes piercing yet not unkind.

"Thank you so much," you manage to stammer out, your voice a mix of relief and lingering fear. "This place is terrifyingly strange."

"Worry not," she replies with a reassuring tone, guiding you towards a door that seems to have materialized from nowhere. As you step through the doorway, a wave of disorientation washes over you, the world spinning in a dizzying blur of colors and sensations.

◉ <u>Continue</u> (Page 23)

After what feels like an eternity spent inside the hollow log, your breath finally steadies, the rapid beating of your heart slowing to a more sustainable rhythm. You cautiously inch towards the opening, your movements deliberate but tense. Peering out into the forest, you hope to catch a glimpse of your surroundings and, more importantly, to confirm whether the Shadow is still lurking nearby.

But as you try to be stealthy, a branch cracks under your slight movement, a sound that, in the oppressive silence of the forest, feels as loud as a gunshot. Your heart, which had just calmed, leaps into your throat.

And then you see it: the Shadow. It's closer than you thought, its form shifting and undulating in the dim light. Upon noticing your movement, the Shadow emits a sound that chills you to the core – a wail that is both sad and agonizing, as if it's in as much pain as it inflicts. The noise reverberates through the trees, a mournful echo that seems to linger in the air.

Panic sets in. You know you can't stay hidden any longer. With a burst of adrenaline, you scramble out of the log, almost tripping over your own feet in your haste. You hit the path running, the underbrush and overhanging branches blurring past as you make a snap decision on which way to go.

Ahead, the path forks in two, each route offering no clues as to where it might lead. The path to the right appears narrower and more overgrown, suggesting it might be less traveled. The denser foliage provide better cover, or might it hinder your escape. The path to the left is a wider and clearer route. It seems more inviting, but that could make it a more obvious choice for the Shadow to follow.

Then again, there's always the option to turn and fight the Shadow. With your back against the wall, maybe confrontation is the only option left.

- ⦿ <u>Take the path to the left.</u> (Page 36)

- ⦿ <u>Take the path to the right.</u> (Page 35)

- ⦿ <u>Turn and fight the Shadow.</u> (Page 33)

As the Shadow's chilling presence draws ever nearer, you feel a surge of primal fear that commands every fiber of your being. Your breath turns ragged, the air in your lungs burning as you draw in one last, desperate gulp. Then, with all the strength and terror surging within you, you release an ear-piercing scream into the darkness, a futile but defiant challenge to the encroaching horror.

The scent of decay invades your senses, a foul, suffocating odor that seems to emanate from the Shadow itself. It's so close now that you can almost feel the icy touch of death. Your heart pounds violently against your ribcage, threatening to burst from the sheer intensity of your fear.

Suddenly, a pressure against your chest sends a jolt of panic through you, and in a reflexive, last-ditch effort to resist your fate, you lash out wildly. Your arms flail, seeking to fend off the imminent doom, but they only meet resistance, tangling and thrashing in a chaotic dance of despair. With one final, guttural scream, you force your eyes open, ready to confront the end.

But instead of the Shadow's ghastly visage, you're met with the familiar surroundings of your bedroom. You're lying in your bed, wrapped in the twisted confines of your comforter, your body slick with sweat.

◉ <u>Continue</u> (Page 58)

Gasping for air, you try to steady your racing heart, the remnants of the nightmare still clawing at the edges of your consciousness.

Glancing at your cell phone, the glowing numbers display 4:30 am, a stark reminder of the real world waiting outside your nightmarish ordeal. Your mind drifts to the unfinished project, the looming exhaustion of the day ahead, and the frustrating realization that sleep has now become an elusive companion.

With a deep, resigned breath, you let your head fall back onto the pillow, the weight of disappointment heavy in your chest. Today is going to be a struggle, a day overshadowed by the remnants of fear and the unyielding demands of reality. You close your eyes, hoping for a few more moments of rest, however futile, before facing the day that you already know is going to be tough.

The End

Approaching the old tractor, you can't help but be drawn to its rusting frame, a relic of forgotten days. Nature has reclaimed much of it; grass and weeds have entwined themselves through the engine block, a testament to the years of neglect. The seat, once perhaps a bright and vibrant red, is now little more than tattered remnants, the padding long since succumbed to the elements.

As you peer closer, curiosity guiding your actions, you notice a small nest tucked away in the engine block. It's a hodgepodge of wilderness and scrap - sticks, twigs, and shredded papers intermingled with bits of fir. The papers seem intriguing, remnants of a human touch amidst the wildness. You wonder about their origin - could they be fragments of a forgotten letter, pages from a diary, or just random scraps discarded without thought?

However, as you sift through the nest, it becomes clear that it's currently uninhabited, the inhabitants likely moved on to a safer, more secluded home. The tractor, for all its intrigue, offers no further clues, leaving you with more questions than answers.

With the tractor explored and yielding little in the way of discovery, you're left considering your next move in this mysterious clearing. The derelict cottage looms nearby, its peeling paint and sagging roofline suggesting a trove of long-forgotten stories. Could its decrepit walls hold the secrets of this place?

Alternatively, the entrance to the root cellar, partially hidden by overgrown vegetation, presents a more ominous allure. Its darkened entrance seems to beckon you, offering a glimpse into the underground mysteries that it might hold.

Or perhaps the woods themselves call to you, their dense canopy and shadowy paths promising further adventure and untold secrets just beyond the clearing.

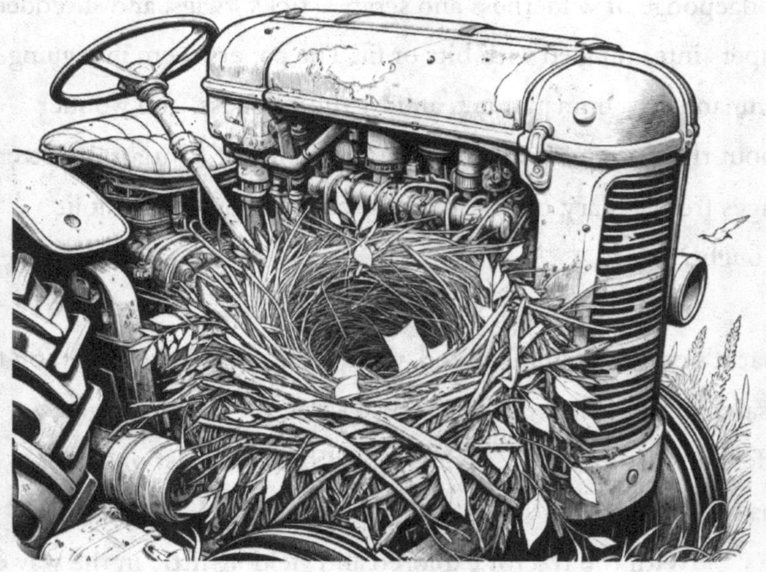

- <u>Investigate the cottage.</u> (Page 62)

- <u>Investigate the root cellar.</u> (Page 63)

- <u>Investigate the tree.</u> (Page 61)

- <u>Leave and explore the woods.</u> (Page 64)

As you gaze upwards, your eyes lock with those of a small grey squirrel perched among the branches. Its bushy tail flicks gently as it observes you, bright eyes reflecting a curious intelligence. The squirrel, with its soft grey fur and nimble movements, appears friendly, but you remind yourself that it's a creature of the wild. Its demeanor seems more inquisitive than fearful, adding an intriguing layer to this encounter in the woods.

The way the squirrel tilts its head, studying you, suggests a level of awareness that piques your interest. It's perched comfortably on a sturdy branch, well out of reach, yet it doesn't seem in any hurry to scamper away. Instead, it sits there, almost as if it's evaluating you, waiting to see your next move in this unexpected meeting.

You consider your options in dealing with this small woodland inhabitant. Its presence, though seemingly mundane, feels like it could be significant in the grand tapestry of the forest's life.

- <u>Chase the squirrel from the tree.</u> (Page 65)

- <u>Ignore the squirrel.</u> (Page 66)

- <u>Talk to the squirrel.</u> (Page 67)

As you navigate through the cluttered room, the sound of sticks cracking underfoot punctuates the eerie silence. You're keenly aware of the contrast between the once-inhabited space and its current state of abandonment. The couch, which should be a symbol of comfort and home, now serves as a playground for a small, unexpected visitor.

Reaching the couch, you see the source of the earlier scurrying - a small gray squirrel perched on the armrest. It has paused in its exploration, now turning its full attention to you. There's a sense of intelligence in its bright, alert eyes, and its tiny paws are poised as if it's ready to leap away at any moment. Despite its apparent curiosity, you remember that this is indeed a wild creature, its behaviors unpredictable.

The squirrel's presence in this dilapidated room adds to the surreal nature of your surroundings. It watches you with an intensity that seems almost human, a tiny guardian of the forgotten space.

You ponder how to handle this unusual encounter. The squirrel, while seemingly innocuous, might react unexpectedly to your actions.

- <u>Chase the squirrel from the room.</u> (Page 69)

- <u>Ignore the squirrel.</u> (Page 71)

- <u>Talk to the squirrel.</u> (Page 73)

As you cautiously make your way down the dark staircase, each step creaks under your weight, echoing through the stillness like a warning. The air grows cooler and damper as you descend, the musty smell of earth and age filling your nostrils. When you finally reach the bottom, you find yourself in a dimly lit room that sends a shiver down your spine.

The room, which appears to be a root cellar, is lined with shelves that reach from floor to ceiling. Each shelf is packed with root boxes, some old and covered in a thick layer of dust, suggesting they haven't been touched in years. The contents are hidden from view, but the sickly odor suggests their contents are long past their use-by date.

In the center of the room stands an old wooden trunk. Its surface is scratched and worn, the wood faded from years of use and neglect. The trunk could contain anything from harmless keepsakes to valuable secrets from the past.

Behind the trunk, adding to the cellar's enigmatic atmosphere, is a heavy wooden door. It looks sturdy, with iron bands reinforcing its structure. It's shut tight, and you can't help but feel curious about what lies beyond. Could it be simply a storage space, or perhaps something more intriguing or sinister?

- ◉ <u>Investigate the old chest.</u> (Page 75)

- ◉ <u>Try the door.</u> (Page 76)

- ◉ <u>Leave the cellar.</u> (Page 77)

As you meander through the tranquil woods, you come upon a breathtaking field, a natural sanctuary bathed in sunlight. The warmth of the sun caresses your back, its golden rays a gentle embrace that fills you with a sense of peace. Here, beside a serene pond, the world feels simpler, more harmonious.

The pond itself is a mirror to the sky, its surface reflecting the fluffy white clouds drifting lazily above. You sit by its edge, lost in the beauty of this idyllic spot. The gentle rustling of the grass and the soft murmur of the water create a symphony of nature's tranquility.

A pair of deer gracefully prance through the field, their movements a dance of elegance and freedom. Their presence adds to the field's charm, a reminder of the natural world's beauty and simplicity. Nearby, a small bunny hops tentatively to the water's edge, its nose twitching as it takes a cautious sip. Watching these gentle creatures, you feel a connection to nature that is both profound and soothing.

As your eyes wander to the edge of the field, they settle on the dark forest that borders this haven. The trees there stand tall and dense, their branches weaving a canopy that casts deep shadows on the forest floor.

- <u>Stay in the well-lit field.</u> (Page 23)

- <u>Explore the forest.</u> (Page 79)

Surrounded by the gentle embrace of nature, you find a playful spirit rising within you. Facing the squirrel perched on the branch, you utter a whimsical "Oogidy Boogidy" and contort your face into an array of silly expressions. It's a light-hearted moment, a small connection to the carefree joys of childhood.

The squirrel, with its bright, observant eyes, watches your antics with what seems like a keen interest. It remains perched, its tiny body perfectly balanced on the slender branch. Then, it begins to chitter, a rapid series of sounds that fill the air with a sense of merriment. Its small hands, dexterous and quick, move to cover its face, and you can't help but interpret the action as laughter. The idea of a squirrel finding amusement in your playful foolishness brings a smile to your face.

This unexpected interaction with the squirrel adds a layer of whimsy to your already peaceful surroundings. The forest around you is alive with the soothing sounds of nature, the rustling leaves, and the gentle breeze creating a serene symphony. The sunlight filters through the canopy, casting dappled patterns of light and shadow around you.

- <u>Throw something.</u> (Page 81)

- <u>Ignore the squirrel.</u> (Page 66)

- <u>Talk to the squirrel.</u> (Page 67)

Respecting the wildness of the forest and its inhabitants, you choose to leave the squirrel to its own devices. There's a certain wisdom in recognizing the boundaries between the human world and the natural one, and you feel at peace with this decision. The squirrel, for its part, continues to chatter and play on its branch, a small but vibrant part of the forest's tapestry.

As you step back from the tree, the serene beauty of your surroundings envelops you once more. The sunlight streams through the leaves in golden beams, casting a warm, dappled light on the forest floor. The air is fresh and fragrant with the scents of earth and foliage, and the gentle rustling of leaves in the breeze creates a soothing backdrop.

Now, as you stand in this tranquil woodland, you ponder your next course of action. There are several paths you could take, each offering its own experience and potential discoveries.

- <u>Investigate the cottage.</u> (Page 62)

- <u>Investigate the root cellar.</u> (Page 63)

- <u>Leave and explore the woods.</u> (Page 64)

In this run-down living room, surrounded by broken furniture and peeling paint, a moment of light-heartedness unfolds as you engage with the small grey squirrel. You utter "Oogidy Boogidy" in a playful tone and pull a series of funny faces, hoping to elicit a reaction. The room around you is bathed in a a dim light shining through the dirt-crusted windows, small dust motes float through the air.

The squirrel, perched comfortably on the arm of an old couch, watches your antics with keen interest. It remains still for a moment, its fluffy tail curled neatly around its body. Then, it begins to chitter, a series of high-pitched sounds that resonate softly in the quiet of the forest. You can't help but notice how its tiny hands move to cover its face, resembling a human gesture of amusement. The scene is endearing, and a part of you is convinced that the squirrel is indeed laughing at your playful display.

In the dilapidated living room of the cottage, a scene of unexpected whimsy unfolds amidst the decay. The room, with its broken furniture and peeling paint, has an air of forgotten stories, yet in this moment, it plays host to a lighter, more amusing chapter. The squirrel, perched on the arm of a weathered couch, becomes a symbol of nature reclaiming this man-made space.

Sunlight streams through the broken windows, casting patterns on the faded walls and floor, mimicking the dappled light of a forest glade. The contrast between the room's rundown state and the squirrel's lively presence creates a unique atmosphere, one that is surprisingly comforting. It's as if the outside world, with its vibrant nature, has crept into this forgotten place, breathing into it a sense of life and gentle humor.

The air in the room feels surprisingly fresh, a faint hint of pine drifting in from the open window, blending with the musty scent of old wood and dust. This combination of aromas gives the room a rustic charm, reminiscent of a forest cabin long left to the whims of nature.

- <u>Throw something.</u> (Page 85)
- <u>Ignore the squirrel.</u> (Page 71)
- <u>Talk to the squirrel.</u> (Page 73)

In the worn-out living room of the abandoned cottage, you decide to honor the presence of the small squirrel without interfering. There's a poignant beauty in observing this wild creature making itself at home amidst the decay. The squirrel, perched on the arm of a faded, threadbare couch, continues to chatter animatedly, its lively spirit a stark contrast to the room's dereliction.

Peeling paint hangs from the walls in ragged strips, and broken furniture lies scattered around, each piece telling a story of neglect. Sunlight filters through cracked and dirt-smudged windows, casting a soft, melancholic glow that highlights the dust motes dancing in the air. The play of light creates a dappled pattern on the floor, reminiscent of sunlight filtering through forest leaves.

The air in the room carries a musty, forgotten scent, but it's punctuated by a subtle freshness that drifts in through the open windows, bringing with it whispers of the world outside. This combination of indoor decay and the persisting life outside creates an atmosphere of calm introspection.

Standing amidst the remnants of what once was someone's home, you take a moment to ponder your next move. In the midst of the run-down and deserted cottage, you find yourself at a crossroads, each option promising its own unique experience:

To your right is the kitchen, a space where once, meals were prepared and perhaps families gathered. Now, the room might hold remnants of its past - rusted appliances, empty shelves, and forgotten utensils or crockery.

There is a door in the back left of the room leading to what was probably a study. An old desks and bookshelves burdened with layers of dust line the walls, silent witnesses to the lives and stories that unfolded in this now-abandoned space.

On the other side of the room, a door to the bedroom hangs from its hinges. What remains of the bed, wardrobe, and personal belongings lay thrown about.

Behind you is the door to the porch and the forest beyond. Wandering in the forest could provide a welcome contrast to the decay within the cottage, offering a sense of freedom and a connection to the wild.

- ⦿ <u>Go into the kitchen.</u> (Page 87)

- ⦿ <u>Go into the office.</u> (Page 105)

- ⦿ <u>Go into the bedroom.</u> (Page 90)

- ⦿ <u>Leave the cottage.</u> (Page 64)

In the musty living room of the run-down cottage, where time and neglect have left their marks, an unexpected and whimsical conversation takes place. The faded wallpaper peels from the walls, and dust motes dance in the slivers of light streaming through the broken windows. Amidst this scene of decay, on the arm of a worn-out couch, sits a small grey squirrel, the unlikely companion in your current dialogue.

You look at the squirrel, a sense of playfulness overtaking you despite the surroundings. "Hi there, squirrel," you say with a chuckle, your voice tinged with a playful silliness, "how are you doing?" Talking to a squirrel feels a bit foolish, especially in the eerie quiet of the abandoned cottage, but the absurdity of it all brings a lightness to your heart.

The squirrel cocks its head, regarding you with beady, intense eyes. It's a curious sight against the backdrop of the derelict room. You laugh softly at yourself, ready to dismiss this silly moment, when suddenly, a clear voice stops you.

"I have a name, you know?"

You spin around, your eyes wide in shock. The squirrel, now standing on its hind legs with tiny hands on its hips, looks at you expectantly. This surreal scene, a talking squirrel in a forgotten living room, leaves you momentarily speechless.

"I'm sorry," you finally reply, disbelief coloring your tone, "did you say something?"

"I did," the squirrel answers, a hint of annoyance in its voice.

Your mind races to process this bizarre encounter. "I just didn't realize squirrels could talk."

"I can," he responds, rolling his eyes in a remarkably human gesture. "And I have a name."

Still grappling with the surreal nature of this conversation, you ask, "Oh, it's good to meet you. What should I call you?"

"My name is Gray," the squirrel says, extending a tiny paw towards you.

⦿ <u>Back away and leave the squirrel.</u> (Page 91)

⦿ <u>Shake the squirrel's hand.</u> (Page 84)

As you step closer to the old wooden chest in the corner of the room, its presence seems almost out of place amidst the decay of the cottage. The chest itself is a relic of craftsmanship, its dark wood weathered by time yet still exuding an air of sturdiness. What truly catches your eye is the intricate ironwork that adorns it — delicate swirls and patterns that speak of an era long gone, a time when such detail was a mark of care and skill.

The lock, an impressive piece of metalwork about three inches square and an inch thick, immediately draws your attention. Despite its age, it gleams with an unexpected luster, free from any trace of rust or decay. It's a small mystery in itself, how something so old could remain in such pristine condition. The lock, solid and seemingly impenetrable, secures the chest firmly, hinting at valuables or secrets hidden within.

The air around you is still, the only sound being the soft creak of the floorboards under your feet. The shafts of light streaming through the windows lay a pattern of light and shadow across the chest, enhancing its mystique. You're struck by a sense of history, of stories untold and treasures possibly forgotten.

- <u>Try to break the lock.</u> (Page 93)

- <u>Search the root cellar.</u> (Page 94)

- <u>Ignore the chest.</u> (Page 76)

You move past the trunk, with its locked secrets, and find yourself drawn toward the heavy wooden door at the back of the room. The door stands as a silent guardian, its surface aged and worn, the wood darkened by years of exposure to the elements within the cottage. Iron bands reinforce it, and the handle, made of wrought iron, looks as old as the door itself.

As you approach, a faint, muffled sound catches your attention. It's a soft, rhythmic sobbing, barely audible but unmistakably human. The realization that someone could be behind this door in such a forgotten and forlorn place sends a shiver down your spine. The cottage, already shrouded in an air of mystery, now takes on an even more curious aspect.

Who could be crying behind this door? Is it a person in distress, or could it be something else – perhaps a trick of the wind or the creaking of the old building? The thought that you're not alone in this abandoned place, that someone, or something, is just on the other side of the wood, heightens your senses and piques your curiosity.

- <u>Try the handle.</u> (Page 95)

- <u>Talk through the door.</u> (Page 96)

- <u>Ignore the door.</u> (Page 77)

You ascend the thin stone staircase heading toward the rectangle of sunlight. You know that something still doesn't feel right about that root cellar. You look back over your shoulder, down the stairs leading into the darkness, and know, as much as you don't want to, you will probably have to go back down into the root cellar. As you emerge from the darkness, you squint your eyes as they adjust to the bright light of day.

Emerging from the root cellar, you take a deep breath, filling your lungs with the fresh, earthy air of the forest. It's a welcome change from the musty, confined space you've just left behind. The sun filters through the canopy above, casting a kaleidoscope of light and shadow on the forest floor. It's a scene of natural beauty, a stark contrast to the enclosed darkness of the cellar.

In front of you, the cottage stands as a silent witness to times past. Its windows, broken and empty, gaze out like soulless eyes, and the door hangs open, an invitation or a warning. The building, with its peeling paint and weathered wood, holds an eerie allure. It's as if the cottage itself is urging you to uncover its secrets, to delve into the stories held within its crumbling walls.

To your left, the path winds back into the depths of the forest. The trees, ancient and towering, seem to huddle close, their branches intertwining to create a canopy that dapples the ground with shades of green and gold. The path promises a journey into the heart of the forest, a return to the wild that you briefly left behind. There's a sense of freedom in the open trail, an escape from the claustrophobic confines of the root cellar. Yet, you remember the Shadow that drove you to the cottage – a lurking presence that adds an undercurrent of danger to the forest's tranquility.

- <u>Explore the cottage.</u> (Page 62)
- <u>Explore the forest.</u> (Page 64)

Under the tree, your brows knit together in a frown as irritation begins to bubble up inside you, mixing uneasily with the underlying current of fear. The squirrel, perched above you, seems almost to be mocking your plight. Desperate to get it out of the tree, you scan the ground for something, anything that could help. Your eyes land on the fallen apples scattered around the base of the tree. They seem to be your only option.

Picking up one of the apples, you assess its weight and firmness. It feels solid and heavy enough in your hand, a suitable choice for your purpose. With a mix of determination and annoyance, you pull your arm back, ready to launch the apple at the squirrel. The action feels drastic, but the situation seems to demand it.

Just as you throw the apple with all your might, aiming for the branch where the squirrel sits, it moves. The squirrel is surprisingly agile, its movements quick and fluid. It easily dodges the incoming apple and, in an unexpected turn of events, leaps towards you.

In that split second, fear overtakes you. The squirrel, now airborne, is heading straight for your face. You let out an involuntary scream, a reaction to the sudden attack. Instinctively, you throw your hands up in front of your face to protect yourself. The thought of the small, wild creature with its sharp claws and teeth coming into contact with your skin sends a wave of panic through you.

Your heart races, and adrenaline floods your system as you brace for the impact. The once calm and peaceful forest setting has turned into a scene of chaos and fear, all because of one small but surprisingly bold squirrel.

- <u>Continue</u> (Page 58)

As you navigate the cluttered room, the sound of sticks cracking underfoot echoes in the eerie silence, a stark reminder of the disarray that now defines the space. The room, once a place of warmth and life, stands in stark contrast to its former self. Furniture lies scattered and abandoned, each piece a testament to the passage of time and neglect.

The couch, in particular, draws your attention. Once a centerpiece of comfort and relaxation, it now sits forlorn and faded. Its fabric is worn and torn, the cushions sagging under the weight of years of disuse.

Where once there might have been the hustle and bustle of a family home, now there is only the quiet decay of a forgotten place. The air is still, heavy with dust and the faint, musty scent of old wood.

You stand in the middle of this room, taking in the scene around you. The peeling wallpaper, the broken window panes letting in shafts of light, the overall sense of decay – it all paints a picture of a once-loved space now relegated to the annals of memory.

- <u>Go into the kitchen.</u> (Page 87)

- <u>Go into the office.</u> (Page 105)

- <u>Go into the bedroom.</u> (Page 90)

- <u>Leave the cottage.</u> (Page 64)

As you cautiously extend your hand towards Gray, there's a moment of surreal anticipation. The sensation of shaking a squirrel's hand is as peculiar as you'd imagine. Gray's tiny paw is surprisingly dexterous as it meets your finger, a soft, delicate touch that's almost feather-like. You can feel the subtle pressure of his small digits, a gentle but firm grasp that conveys a sense of intelligence and awareness far beyond what one would expect from a woodland creature.

"Hi, Gray," you say, a smile spreading across your face as you engage in this unusual greeting. It's a bizarre yet charming moment, a handshake bridging the gap between the human world and the wild. "Your house?" you ask, still holding onto the wonder of the handshake.

"Yup," Gray responds with a proud flick of his bushy tail, his tiny mouth curving into what resembles a smile. "I came by here a while ago and no one was here, so I moved in. Like it?" Your eyes wander over the scene – the rusted tractor, the overgrown grass, and the cottage that wears its age like a badge of honor. Despite the apparent disrepair, there's a whimsical charm to the place, a sense of life amidst the decay, much like the small, handshaking squirrel who now calls it home.

- <u>Say it looks nice.</u> (Page 99)
- <u>Call it a dump.</u> (Page 101)

As you step into the kitchen of the abandoned cottage, the scene is both comical and slightly unnerving. The once-functional kitchen is now a playground for the local wildlife, evidenced by the state of disarray before you. The open shelves, which perhaps once proudly displayed dishes and glassware, are now host to a collection of boxes. Each box looks worn and nibbled at the edges, clear signs of a rodent's frequent visits.

The countertops, which should be the heart of kitchen activity, are instead littered with an assortment of old leaves and sticks. These natural debris, seemingly out of place in the indoor setting, have been carelessly strewn across the surface, likely the work of the same creature responsible for the chewed boxes.

As your eyes scan the room, a sudden movement on one of the shelves captures your attention. You inch closer, curiosity piqued, and there it is – the small grey squirrel. It sits contentedly, its head buried in one of the boxes, seemingly oblivious to the chaos it has wrought in its search for food or nesting materials. The squirrel chitters away in a rhythm that sounds almost like laughter, adding a layer of humor to the peculiar situation.

The squirrel's nonchalant demeanor in the midst of the mess it has created is both amusing and frustrating. You find yourself caught between laughing at the absurdity of it all and feeling annoyed by the sheer cheek of the little intruder.

The squirrel, still rummaging through the box, suddenly pauses and turns its head towards you. For a moment, it regards you with those bright, inquisitive eyes, and you can almost sense a mischievous glint in them. Then, with a swift movement that catches you off guard, it reaches into the box and flings a handful of old cereal in your direction.

The cereal scatters in the air, some of it landing on your head and shoulders. The squirrel tilts its head, and in a surprisingly articulate voice, it says, "Get out of my house."

You stand there, slightly stunned, bits of stale cereal clinging to your hair. The absurdity of being scolded by a squirrel in a dilapidated kitchen adds an almost surreal quality to the experience. A small part of you admires the creature's boldness and wit.

- <u>Apologize to the squirrel.</u> (Page 102)
- <u>Ignore the squirrel.</u> (Page 91)
- <u>Leave the room.</u> (Page 104)

As the first rays of morning filter through the trees, you awaken amidst the forest's embrace. You sit up, brushing leaves from your tousled hair, feeling a surprising energy despite the makeshift nature of your bed. You survey your modest campsite, the warm, smoldering coals of your small fire glow faintly in your makeshift fire-pit, a testament to your survival skills.

Beside you lies a wooden staff, its design a blend of practicality and artistry, somewhere between a walking stick and a weapon. As your hand wraps around its handle, a rush of comfortable familiarity floods through you. The staff feels like an extension of yourself, its weight and balance perfect in your grip.

Though you don't remember coming here or even where 'here' is, an intrinsic part of you seems to understand. You feel a compelling urge to walk west. It's as if a path is laid out before you, leading to others who share your calling.

You stand up, a sense of pride swelling in your chest. You're a hunter of Shadows, a guardian in this mysterious world. The idea that there are others like you out there, those who also protect the denizens and wanderers of this realm, fills you with hope and determination.

The End

As you step over the threshold into the room the aroma of mold is strong, a testament to the years of neglect the cottage has endured. This musty scent is oddly intertwined with the lingering essence of pipe smoke, a remnant of a time when this room was perhaps a haven of relaxation and contemplation.

Pulling the collar of your shirt up to cover your nose and mouth, you cautiously move further into the room. Each step feels heavy, as if the very air is saturated with the memories and secrets of the past. The light here is dim, filtering through curtains heavy with dust, casting the room in a subdued, almost sepulchral glow.

The furnishings are sparse and speak of a simpler time. A modest dresser stands against one wall, its surface layered with dust and the paint peeling in places. Beside it, a nightstand holds a single, unlit candle, its wax discolored with age. The bed, situated in the center of the room, is covered with a moth-eaten blanket, the fabric worn thin in spots, revealing the faded patterns of a bygone era.

- <u>Go into the kitchen.</u> (Page 91)

- <u>Go into the office.</u> (Page 105)

- <u>Leave the cottage.</u> (Page 64)

Motivated by a mix of curiosity and determination, you scour the room for something to break the stubborn lock. Amidst the rubble and decay, your eyes catch a loose rock, partially buried under debris. It's hefty and rough, with jagged edges that suggest it might be just the tool you need.

You grasp the rock firmly, feeling its cold weight in your hand. You position the rock against the lock, ready to strike. The anticipation of what secrets might be hidden inside sends a thrill through you. With a deep breath, you swing the rock hard against the lock.

The sound of metal clashing against stone echoes through the root cellar, unnaturally loud in the stillness. You strike again, more forcefully this time, the sound reverberating off the walls.

Suddenly, the eerie quiet of the room is shattered by another sound — something shifting, moving from the doorway at the end of the room. Your heart skips a beat as you realize you're not alone. From the darkness, a form emerges, something undefined and shifting, a presence that feels both sinister and intangible — a Shadow advances, an oppressive sense of dread filling the room.

- Throw a rock at the Shadow:
  <u>One</u> or <u>Two</u> (Page 107 or 109)

- <u>Cower in fear.</u> (Page 37)

- <u>Run away.</u> (Page 64)

A sense of unease grips you. The air is thick and damp, the kind that clings to your skin and fills your lungs with an earthy, rotting scent. The only light comes from a dim bulb hanging precariously from a frayed wire above, casting eerie shadows on the walls.

The shelves of the cellar are lined with boxes, their contents hidden under a layer of time and neglect. As you gingerly open each box, your hands meet the unpleasant texture of slimy, decaying roots. The sight and feel of them make your stomach churn, their once vibrant life now reduced to a mushy, unrecognizable mass. Each box seems to hold a similar fate, a grim reminder of the passage of time and the inevitable end of all things.

As you continue your search, hoping to find a key to the mysterious chest upstairs, a muffled sound from the back room of the cellar catches your attention. It's faint, but in the silence of the cellar, it echoes like a whisper of something sinister. The sound is indistinct, yet it carries a sense of urgency that sends a chill down your spine.

Your heart races as you weigh your options, the atmosphere in the cellar growing more oppressive by the minute.

- <u>Try to break the lock.</u> (Page 93)

- <u>Investigate the door.</u> (Page 76)

- <u>Explore the cottage.</u> (Page 62)

"Thank you for saying that," Gray remarks, his bushy tail flicking thoughtfully as he surveys the room with a discerning eye. His voice, surprisingly articulate for a squirrel, carries a hint of humor despite acknowledging the cottage's state of disrepair. "But we both know it's not the nicest place to live."

His fur, a rich shade of gray with streaks of darker tones, bristles slightly as he turns, giving him a look of curious intelligence. You chuckle softly, finding his blend of frankness and charm endearing. "You looked so proud of it, I wanted to be nice."

Gray cocks his head, the motion causing his small, rounded ears to twitch. His bright, inquisitive eyes reflect a newfound respect as he considers your words. "I like you," he declares with a sincerity that belies his small stature. "I think I'm going to come along with you."

Before you can respond, Gray leaps nimbly from his perch onto your shoulder. His small, furry body is warm against your neck, and you feel the gentle tickle of his tail as he finds his balance. The texture of his fur is soft and well-kept, a sign of his resourcefulness and adaptability. The unexpected closeness of this little woodland creature is surprisingly comforting, and a sense of companionship washes over you. It's nice to have a friend, even if it's a small talking squirrel, in this strange and abandoned place.

"Alright," you agree, a smile forming as you're buoyed by Gray's presence. "Let's see what else is around here."

With Gray now your official companion, the exploration of the cottage takes on a new, more cheerful tone. His tiny claws grip your shirt gently, ensuring he's secure as you both prepare to uncover the hidden mysteries and stories within the peeling walls and creaky floors of the cottage.

- <u>Go into the kitchen.</u> (Page 115)

- <u>Go into the office.</u> (Page 121)

- <u>Go into the bedroom.</u> (Page 117)

- <u>Leave the cottage.</u> (Page 122)

You look around at the crumbling walls and the debris scattered around, unable to hold back your true thoughts. "Honestly, it's kind of a dump," you admit, more bluntly than you intended.

At your words, Gray's demeanor changes instantly. His bushy tail, once flicking playfully, now droops in disappointment. The brightness in his eyes dims, and he looks away, clearly hurt by your candid assessment.

"I thought you were different," he says, his voice tinged with sadness. With a heavy heart, he leaps from his perch, landing softly on the ground. Without another word or glance, Gray scurries away, disappearing into the shadows.

You're left standing alone, regretting the impact of your words. The room feels emptier without Gray's lively presence. You realize that your blunt honesty might have cost you a unique and valuable friendship in this lonely, forgotten place.

- <u>Go into the kitchen.</u> (Page 91)

- <u>Go into the office.</u> (Page 105)

- <u>Go into the bedroom.</u> (Page 90)

- <u>Leave the cottage.</u> (Page 64)

As you stand in the dilapidated kitchen of the abandoned cottage, you brush the remnants of stale cereal off your shoulders. The oddity of the situation brings a sheepish smile to your face. "I'm sorry," you say, your voice tinged with genuine remorse. "I didn't mean to intrude. It's actually a nice place you've got here, considering."

Gray, the small grey squirrel with a bushy tail that seems too large for his tiny body, cocks his head to the side. His bright eyes, surrounded by tufts of softer gray fur, study you with a mix of skepticism and curiosity. "Nice? You really think so?" he asks, his voice clear and articulate, a trait that still catches you off guard.

The kitchen, with its peeling paint and aged cupboards hanging askew, is bathed in the soft light filtering through the grimy window. Spiderwebs adorn the corners, and the once-white tiles are now a faded yellow, each crack and chip telling a story of the past.

"Well, it has character," you reply, attempting to lighten the mood. The room, despite its decay, holds a peculiar charm, enhanced by Gray's presence.

"Thank you for saying that," Gray responds, his tail twitching as he takes in the surroundings with a discerning eye. His voice, laced with humor, acknowledges the cottage's obvious wear and tear. "But we both know it's not the nicest place to live."

Your laughter is soft, a sound that seems out of place in kitchen. "You looked so proud of it, I wanted to be ension in the air seems to lift, and you add, "I could ound here. How about we explore this place

Gray ponders your offer for a brief moment before nodding. "I'd like that," he agrees, his small paws padding softly as he scampers down from his perch and joins you on the ground.

Now accompanied by Gray, you feel a renewed sense of curiosity and excitement about uncovering the mysteries hidden within the cottage's walls. The kitchen, with its faded glory, is just the beginning.

- <u>Explore the kitchen.</u> (Page 115)

- <u>Go to the office.</u> (Page 121)

- <u>Go into the bedroom.</u> (Page 117)

- <u>Leave the cottage.</u> (Page 122)

Emerging from the kitchen, the stillness of the c[o]
envelops you, a tangible reminder of its abandonment. Befo[re]
you, two doors stand ajar, shrouded in the quiet mystery of w[hat]
beyond. One leads to the office, the other to the bedroom, bot[h]
holding the secrets of a life once lived within these walls.

To your left, the open door to the outside frames a view
of the sunlit world beyond. The sunlight streams in, casting
beams through the floating dust motes that dance in the air, a
silent ballet of light and shadow. It's a stark reminder of the
isolation of the cottage.

The room around you whispers tales of the past.
Furniture, once the heart of a bustling household, now lies
scattered and abandoned. The couch, a sad relic of comfort and
relaxation, is faded and forlorn. Its fabric is tattered, the cushions
sagging, each tear and stain a testament to the relentless march
of time.

In this place where laughter and warmth once echoed,
there is now only the quiet, somber decay of a forgotten past.
The air hangs heavy with the musty scent of old wood and lost
memories. Each creak of the floorboard under your feet seems to
echo through the empty halls.

- <u>Investigate the office.</u> (Page 105)

- <u>Go into the bedroom.</u> (Page 90)

- <u>Leave the cottage.</u> (Page 64)

Stepping into what was once a study or office, a profound sense of desolation washes over you. The room, a stark reminder of the passage of time, is in disarray. The desk, a centerpiece of the room, stands with its drawers ajar, its contents spilled out as if in a hurried search long ago. Among the scattered items, sticks from the surrounding forest have found their way inside, a sign of nature slowly reclaiming the space.

The floor is a mess of small office supplies. Paper clips, pens, and other remnants of a once-ordered life are strewn about in a chaotic tapestry. Each object seems to hold a story, a fragment of a day in the life of someone who once found purpose in this room. The disarray speaks volumes of the abrupt departure of the room's occupant, leaving behind these small tokens of their daily existence.

Amidst the chaos of scattered office supplies, your gaze is drawn to an unsettling sight. Clusters of mold proliferate across the scattered papers around the desk, an insidious infestation that has claimed the room as its own. The mold is not just a simple growth; it has a sinister, almost intentional design. Its colors range from a sickly greenish-grey to splotches of deep black, with occasional flecks of white that seem to pulse and wriggle under the dim light. The patterns it forms are eerily reminiscent of forgotten runes or cryptic symbols, as if the mold is an entity trying to communicate through decay.

The papers, once bearing words and memories, are now half-consumed by this creeping blight, their edges curling and disintegrating under the mold's relentless advance. The very air around it feels tainted, heavy with the musty stench of rot and dampness. This unnatural garden of mold imparts a creeping dread, a physical manifestation of time's unrelenting march and the inevitability of nature's reclamation.

As you survey the mess, a pang of regret courses through you. It's as though the abandoned room reflects a missed opportunity, a path not taken. The scattered pens and paper clips are like echoes of decisions left unmade, actions not taken. This sense of loss, of what might have been, weighs heavily on you. You feel a deep sense of responsibility for not having acted when you had the chance, a realization that your inaction may have cost you more than you ever understood.

With a heavy heart, you turn away from the disheveled office, the remnants of its past life a stark reminder of opportunities missed and paths not taken. The loneliness of the room is palpable, its eerie stillness a silent witness to the transient nature of human endeavors.

- <u>Examine the moldy papers.</u> (Page 121)

- <u>Go into the bedroom.</u> (Page 90)

- <u>Leave the cottage.</u> (Page 64)

The forest around you seems to hold its breath as you frantically search the ground for a rock, any sort of weapon to defend yourself against the looming Shadow. The air is thick with an electric charge of fear and suspense, the usually comforting sounds of the forest now eerily absent. Your fingers finally close around a sizable stone, its rough surface cold and solid in your trembling hand.

The Shadow, a formless mass of darkness and malevolence, towers before you. It raises its spectral claws, which appear more solid than the rest of its shadowy form, poised to strike. You can almost feel the chill emanating from it, a coldness that seeps into your very bones.

In a desperate move, you dodge to the side, the Shadow's claws slicing through the air where your head was just a moment before. Adrenaline surges through you, fueling your movements as you hurl the rock with all your might at the Shadow. The stone cuts through the air, aimed at the heart of the creature.

As the claws descend upon you, a searing pain erupts across your chest. You gasp, the impact knocking the breath from your lungs. In that same instant, your hastily thrown rock connects with its target. There's a moment of surreal clarity as the stone strikes a dark, pulsating heart embedded within the Shadow's chest.

Time seems to slow as the Shadow's form shudders, its essence rippling like disturbed water. The heart, dislodged by the impact of the rock, emits a burst of dark energy. You watch, a mix of pain and awe, as the Shadow begins to dissipate, unraveling like smoke in the wind.

In the clearing, as the Shadow fades, an overwhelming sense of gratitude fills the air. It's as if the forest itself is breathing a sigh of relief. The word 'gratitude' resonates in your mind, echoing as the creature vanishes, leaving you alone in the now peaceful clearing.

As you struggle to catch your breath, the pain in your chest a stark reminder of the encounter, you realize that the immediate danger for the child has passed, but everything has a cost. It seems that you have bought that child's freedom with your own life. You feel the burning in your chest of the Shadow's final swipe and are overcome by exhaustion. You see the kid come out of the bushes and look around, still unable to see you, before he breathes a sigh of relief and, stretching, fades himself.

- <u>Continue</u> (Page 89)

The forest, usually a haven of natural sounds and rhythms, now lies in an oppressive silence as you frantically search the ground. Your fingers, trembling with a mix of fear and determination, finally close around a sizable stone. Its surface is rough, cold, and unyielding – a small comfort in the face of the looming, formless Shadow.

The Shadow, an embodiment of darkness and malevolence, stands towering before you. Its spectral claws, unnervingly solid compared to its shadowy form, are raised menacingly. A palpable chill emanates from it, a coldness that seems to reach into the very marrow of your bones.

In a moment of desperate courage, you lunge to the side, narrowly evading the Shadow's deadly swipe. Your heart pounding, you hurl the rock with all your might at the creature. The stone, however, veers off course, missing the Shadow entirely and disappearing into the dark underbrush.

As the claws of the Shadow descend upon you, a sharp, searing pain tears across your chest. The force of the blow knocks you back, your breath coming in ragged gasps. The world seems to blur at the edges, your vision narrowing as you struggle to remain conscious.

In those fleeting moments of clarity, you see the child break from the bushes, their face etched with fear and relief. The Shadow, now unfettered by your defense, turns its attention towards the child.

You lie there, helplessly watching as the Shadow pursuing the kid with relentless, chilling intent. A sense of despair washes over you, a realization that your sacrifice might have been in vain.

The pain in your chest is a burning reminder of the Shadow's touch, a physical manifestation of the price paid. Exhaustion overwhelms you, your body and mind succumbing to the inevitable. As your consciousness slips away, the forest seems to reclaim its sounds, the natural chorus resuming as if to fill the void left by your departure. The child is still in danger, and all you were able to do with your sacrifice was buy them a few moments respite. You hope that it was enough to let the child escape and wish you could have done more. You close your eyes, surrendering to the embrace of the forest, the word 'gratitude' echoing in your fading thoughts.

⦿ <u>Continue.</u> (Page 123)

The kitchen of the abandoned cottage exudes an air of sinister neglect. As you step through the creaking door, the stale, musty odor of decay hits you, instantly setting your nerves on edge. The once charming space is now a tableau of deterioration. Faded wallpaper peels from the walls in curling strips, and the few remaining cabinets hang open, their hinges rusted and groaning.

Sparse shafts of light filter through the dirt-encrusted windows, casting eerie shadows across the room. The air is heavy and still, as if even the breeze is hesitant to enter this forsaken place. You can't shake off the feeling of being watched, though the cottage appears to be devoid of life.

Your attention is drawn to several boxes of foodstuffs scattered on the counters and the floor. The packaging looks old, the colors faded and the labels peeling. Upon closer inspection, you notice that the corners of these boxes have been nibbled on, tiny bite marks fraying the edges. You recall the squirrel you've seen flitting about the property, its presence now adding a touch of the uncanny to the already unsettling atmosphere.

As you sift through the clutter, something catches your eye—a key with an ornate handle, tied with a faded yellow ribbon. The key is anachronistic, its design harking back to a bygone era. It's heavy in your hand, the metal cool and slightly rusted, the intricate patterns on the handle speaking of craftsmanship rarely seen in modern times.

Holding the key, a wave of unease washes over you. It feels significant, like a piece to a puzzle you didn't know you were assembling. The ribbon, once bright and cheerful, now hangs limp and discolored, as if it too has succumbed to the despondency of the cottage.

Your mind races with questions. What door does this key unlock? What secrets lie hidden behind it? The feeling of being observed intensifies, and the air seems to grow colder. You're torn between the desire to uncover the mysteries of this place and the instinctive urge to flee.

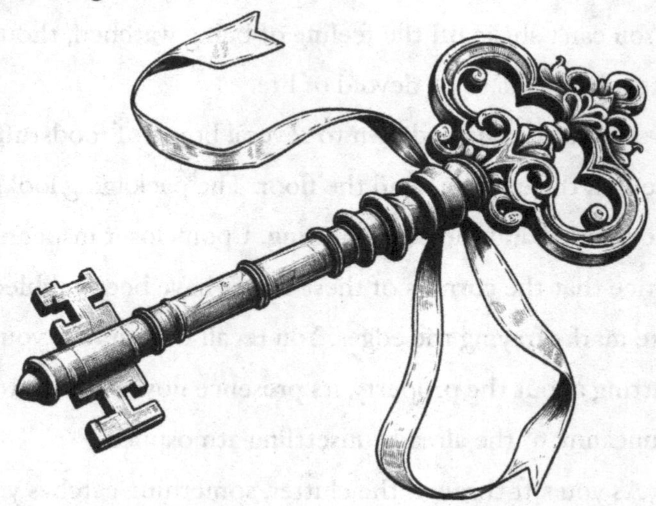

- <u>Go into the bedroom.</u> (Page 90)

- <u>Go into the office.</u> (Page 105)

- <u>Leave the cottage.</u> (Page 125)

The oppressive silence of the forest weighs heavily upon you as you stand, facing the looming Shadow. This dark entity, a formless specter of malice, towers over you, its chilling presence sapping the warmth from the air. Its spectral claws, unnaturally tangible against its nebulous form, hover with a menacing promise of pain.

In a fleeting moment of desperate bravery, you lunge to the side, narrowly escaping the deadly swipe of the Shadow's claws. Your heart races, adrenaline coursing through your veins as you realize there is no stone in your hand, no weapon to defend yourself. You are unarmed, vulnerable.

Acting on instinct and raw courage, you charge at the Shadow, hoping to disrupt its focus or perhaps to give the hidden child a chance to escape. Your efforts, however, are in vain. The Shadow, undeterred by your unarmed attack, easily sidesteps your charge.

The Shadow's claws find their mark, tearing across your chest with a sharp, agonizing pain. You're thrown backward, the force of the attack more than you can bear. Your vision begins to blur, the edges of your consciousness fraying as you struggle to stay awake.

In your last moments of lucidity, you see the child emerge from the bushes, their face a mix of fear and fleeting hope. The Shadow, now unimpeded, turns its malevolent attention towards the child and resumes its pursuit.

Lying on the forest floor, a deep sense of regret and disappointment engulfs you. Your sacrifice, though valiant, feels futile. The child is still in danger, and your intervention has only bought them a brief respite. The burning pain in your chest is a stark reminder of your encounter with the Shadow, a token of your failed attempt to protect.

As the sounds of the forest slowly return, filling the void left by the Shadow's presence, you hope that your efforts were enough to give the child a chance to escape. Lamenting your inability to do more, you close your eyes, succumbing to the inevitable. The word 'gratitude' echoes in your mind, a bitter reminder of your unfulfilled desire to save.

⊙ <u>Continue</u> (Page 123)

he kitchen of the abandoned cottage greets you with its

tillness, and the air is laden with the scent of decay and

memories. Once charming and full of life, the kitchen

 as a testament to the passage of time, with faded

peeling from the walls and cabinets hanging askew,

nges emitting a plaintive groan.

Shafts of light struggle through the grime-coated
ındows, casting ghostly shadows that dance across the room.
The stillness is so profound it feels almost deliberate, as though
the cottage itself is holding its breath, creating a heavy,
oppressive atmosphere.

Amidst the disarray, several boxes of old foodstuffs are
scattered across the counters and floor. Their faded, peeling
labels and frayed, nibbled corners suggest the presence of a small,
mischievous inhabitant. It's then you hear a familiar, playful
chatter of Gray, your new friend.

"Ah, you found my treasure trove!" Gray exclaims, his
bushy tail twitching with excitement as he eyes the boxes. "I've
had quite the feast here, but look what else I found!"

Your eyes follow his gaze to a key lying amidst the clutter.
Its ornate handle and intricate design catch the dim light, casting
a muted glow. Gray hops closer, his bright eyes reflecting the
key's sheen. "Isn't it pretty? I love shiny things! And guess what?
There's another shiny thing like this in the bedroom!"

Despite the kitchen's ominous atmosphere, Gray's enthusiasm brings a momentary lightness to the scene. Hold the key, you feel its significance, its weight hinting at hidden stories waiting to be uncovered. The ribbon, faded from its former glory, adds to the key's mysterious allure.

As you ponder the key's purpose, the chill in the air seems to grow more pronounced, the sense of being watched more acute. Yet, Gray's presence and playful demeanor offer a semblance of comfort in this otherwise foreboding environment.

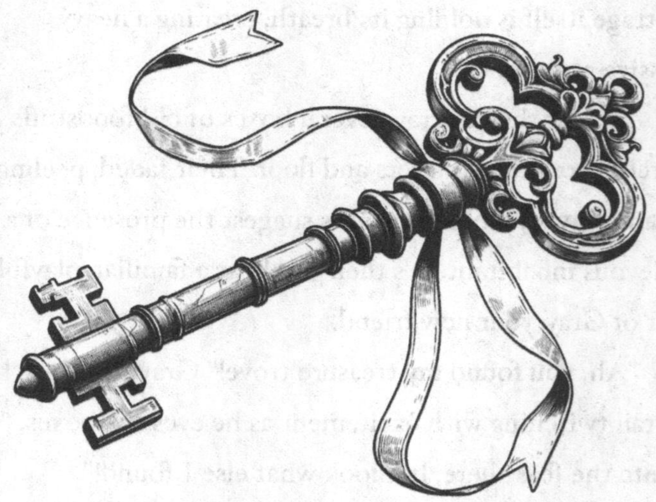

- <u>Go into the bedroom.</u> (Page 119)

- <u>Go into the office.</u> (Page 121)

- <u>Leave the cottage.</u> (Page 126)

As you navigate the musty room, Gray's companionship breaks the eerie stillness. He darts playfully around the room, his bushy tail leaving a trail in the dust.

"Hey there!" Gray chirps, his bright eyes gleaming with mischief. "You look like you could use a bit of fun in this gloomy place. Guess what I found?"

Intrigued by his cheerful demeanor, you can't help but smile. "What did you find, Gray?"

"Something shiny!" he exclaims with glee. "I hid it behind the dresser. It's a game I play – hide and seek with treasures. You should check it out!"

The oppressive atmosphere of the room seems to lift slightly with Gray's playful energy. You approach the dresser, its old wood creaking as you gently move it away from the wall.

"Left a bit... right a bit... there!" Gray directs, his excitement palpable. "You're getting warmer!"

Following his instructions, you finally spot a glimmer behind the dresser. Reaching down, you retrieve an old-fashioned key tied with a red ribbon. Its ornate handle is intricate, and despite its age, it has a certain elegance.

"Wow, Gray, this is amazing!" you exclaim, examining the key. "It's beautiful."

"I know, right? I have an eye for shiny things," Gray boasts proudly.

Holding the key, a sense of accomplishment washes over you. Despite the sinister air of the cottage, Gray's presence has brought a spark of lightness to your exploration.

Gray's expression shifts to a more serious tone. "But hey, don't go into the office, okay? It smells really funny in there. And not the 'ha-ha' kind of funny. More like the 'yuck!' kind."

With the ornate key in your hand and Gray's warning echoing in your mind, a sense of curiosity mixed with caution fills you. Despite the foreboding aura of the cottage, Gray's playful nature adds a touch of lightness to the exploration.

"Alright, Gray, thanks for the heads-up," you reply, chuckling at his description. "Let's get out of here."

With Gray by your side, you feel a bit more at ease as you continue to unravel the mysteries of the cottage, steering clear of the office as advised.

- <u>Go into the office.</u> (Page 121)
- <u>Leave the cottage.</u> (Page 127)

The oppressive heaviness of the room lifts slightly as Gray, the lively squirrel, scampers in behind you. His presence introduces a much-needed lightness to the atmosphere, his tail swishing through the layers of dust.

"Hi there!" Gray chirps, his bright eyes sparkling with mischief. "You look like you're on a serious mission in this old place. But guess what? I found something that'll make it more fun!

Your curiosity piqued, you can't help but smile at his enthusiasm. "What's that, Gray?"

"It's shiny and hidden!" Gray says excitedly. "Behind the dresser. I love hiding things, especially shiny things. You really should see it!"

Motivated by Gray's cheerful demeanor, you carefully move the heavy dresser. With a gentle push, it creaks aside, revealing a hidden spot behind it.

"Right there! You're so close!" Gray guides you eagerly. As you look down, a small shiny object catches your eye.

You reach down and pick up an old-fashioned key with a delicate yellow ribbon tied around it. The key, ornate and elegant, seems to hold stories of the past.

"This is fascinating, Gray," you say, admiring the key. "It's really quite beautiful."

"I know, right? I have a knack for finding shiny things," Gray boasts, his tail twitching happily. "Oh, but don't bother with the office. It smells funny in there, and not the good kind of funny!"

Holding the key, you feel a sense of intrigue and excitement. Despite the eerie atmosphere of the cottage, Gray's playful presence brings a sense of adventure to the air.

Gray's expression shifts to a more serious tone. "But hey, don't go into the office, okay? It smells really funny in there. And not the 'ha-ha' kind of funny. More like the 'yuck!' kind."

With the ornate key in your hand and Gray's warning echoing in your mind, a sense of curiosity mixed with caution fills you. Despite the foreboding aura of the cottage, Gray's playful nature adds a touch of lightness to the exploration.

"Alright, Gray, thanks for the heads-up," you reply, chuckling at his description. "Let's find out what these key opens."

With Gray by your side, you feel a bit more at ease as you continue to unravel the mysteries of the cottage, steering clear of the office as advised.

- ◉ <u>Go into the office.</u> (Page 121)
- ◉ <u>Leave the cottage.</u> (Page 128)

Dawn's early light creeps over the horizon as you stir from an uneasy sleep, the remnants of a strange dream clinging to the edges of your consciousness. You find yourself lying beside a wooden cart, its surface laden with a trove of sparkling gemstones, intricate dreamcatchers, and an array of talismans from cultures near and far.

There's a jade figurine from the Far East, to ward off evil spirits; a turquoise amulet from the Southwest, a stone of protection and strength; and a small pouch filled with runes, each symbol an ancient letter from a Norse alphabet, said to predict the future and guide one's path. A collection of dreamcatchers, with their woven nets and feathered strands, promises to filter the night's dreams.

As you sit up, rubbing the sleep from your eyes, you gaze out at the small town emerging in the soft light of morning. It sits on the edge of a tranquil river whose waters whisper of journeys and secrets untold. You can't quite recall how you came to be here, but flashes of trying to help someone flicker through your mind, a disjointed echo of another place.

Looking down at the cart, your hands pass over the items with practiced ease. Each object has a purpose, a use in the realm of dreams and protection, and you know them all intimately—it is, after all, your cart. You understand these items not just as wares to be sold, but as tools to aid those navigating the unpredictable landscapes of the Dreamworld.

Shaking off the last vestiges of your otherworldly dream —visions of metal carriages that moved without horses—you ready yourself for the day ahead. With a determined grip, you begin wheeling your cart into the center of town, each turn of the wheels a step further into your new reality.

You have not become a Dreamweaver, as you might have thought in your final moments in the other world. When the Shadow claimed you, it unknowingly granted you a new existence. Here, in the Dreamworld, you are known as a caretaker —a noble title for one who dispenses charms and talismans to safeguard the sleepers and travelers within this realm.

Your sacrifice has been transformed into purpose, and as you set up your cart in the heart of the town, you embrace your role. You are a guide, a sentinel, a keeper of peace in the world of dreams. And though it came at a great cost, it is a role you accept with honor and a quiet sense of pride.

The End

The crisp air greets you as you step outside the oppressive confines of the house, washing away the lingering feeling of loneliness that clung to your skin like cobwebs. The brightness of the outside world is a stark contrast to the shadows you've left behind.

Your gaze is drawn to the root cellar, a small wooden door set into the earth off to the left. It seems to call to you, its darkened entrance like the mouth of a cave promising secrets and hidden truths. The air around it is cooler, a draft emanating from the darkness below that smells of damp soil and something you can't quite place—a scent that hints at mysteries buried deep beneath the surface.

To your right, the forest trail winds into the dense thicket of trees, a patchwork of light and shadow. The forest whispers of a different kind of mystery, alive with the rustling of leaves and the distant call of birds. It's inviting in its own way, promising the thrill of discovery and the freedom of the wild.

You pat the key in your pocket, its presence a tangible link to unanswered questions. Behind its corresponding lock could lie the answers you seek, a revelation that might shed light on the uneasy feelings left by the house, or something more—a truth that could alter your perception of everything.

- <u>Descend into the root cellar.</u> (Page 130)

- <u>Leave the cottage.</u> (Page 64)

Stepping out of the house, you're greeted by a burst of fresh air and sunlight, a welcome reprieve from the gloom within. Gray, your chipper squirrel friend, bounds over, his fluffy tail high in excitement.

"Isn't this great?" Gray exclaims, inhaling deeply. "Much better than being cooped up inside!" Then he spots the root cellar. "Hey, check that out!" he says, pointing with a paw. "Bet there's something cool down there!"

"I though you said being outside was better, now you want to go inside again?" You ask, shaking your head.

"What can I say," Gray titters, "there could be something interesting down there.

The forest to your right beckons with its own mysteries, but the key in your pocket and Gray's eager offers you another path.

"Adventure time!" Gray insists, nudging you playfully. "There could be cheese! Or treasures! Let's go!"

- <u>**Descend into the root cellar.**</u> (Page 131)
- <u>**Leave the cottage.**</u> (Page 64)

As you step out of the house, happy to be out of the stifling air. Breathing in the earthen scent mixed with pine of the forest, you enjoy the warmth of the sun beaming down on your shoulders.

"Ah, breathe that in!" Gray chirps, his voice a bubbly melody against the backdrop of the quiet outdoors. "So much better than the stuffy old house, right?"

You glance at the root cellar you noticed on your way in. The small, wooden door set into the earth whispers of secrets and history, the cool draft hinting at hidden things.

"Ooh, what's that?" Gray's voice pulls you from your reverie as he points with his tiny paw toward the cellar. "Looks like adventure! Maybe there's cheese, or... or shiny things! We should totally check it out!"

To your right, the forest trail stretches into a dense thicket of trees. The forest seems to hum with a life of its own, offering a different path, one that promises exploration and the joy of the wild.

- <u>Descend into the root cellar.</u> (Page 133)
- <u>Leave the cottage.</u> (Page 64)

As you step out of the house, the lingering cobwebs of loneliness are swept away by the caress of the fresh air. The sun dapples the ground with light, banishing the shadows that still seem to cling to your memory.

You barely have a moment to appreciate the sharp contrast between the gloom inside and the vibrancy outside when Gray, your ever-cheerful squirrel companion, skitters up to your side. His tail is a fluffy banner waving in the gentle breeze.

"Ah, breathe that in!" Gray chirps, his voice a bubbly melody against the backdrop of the quiet outdoors. "So much better than the stuffy old house, right?"

Your eyes are naturally drawn to the root cellar nearby. The small, wooden door set into the earth whispers of secrets and history, the cool draft beckoning with a hint of damp earth and deep, hidden things.

"Ooh, what's that?" Gray's voice pulls you from your reverie as he points with his tiny paw toward the cellar. "Looks like adventure! Maybe there's cheese, or... or shiny things! We should totally check it out!"

To your right, the forest trail stretches into a dense thicket of trees. The forest seems to hum with a life of its own, offering a different path, one that promises exploration and the joy of the wild.

With the key in your pocket feeling heavier by the moment, you're reminded that every lock awaits its key, and every secret its reveal. The cellar could hold the answers, or perhaps more questions, but the forest offers its own allure, its own potential for discovery.

Gray seems to sense your indecision and nudges your hand with his head, his bright eyes glinting. "Come on, what are we waiting for? Let's go find out what's down there! It'll be fun!" His enthusiasm is infectious, and for a moment, the cellar seems less daunting.

- <u>Descend into the root cellar.</u> (Page 134)

- <u>Leave the cottage.</u> (Page 64)

As you descend a heavy wooden door looms large at the other end of the room. As you approach you can hear muffled sounds of crying from the other side. You slide the key carefully into the large metal lock on the door. It fits perfectly, and turns with a resonant click that echoes through the silent room.

Cautiously you nudge open the door just a sliver. You peer into the dimly lit room beyond. The narrow aperture unleashes a torrent of emotion — fear and sorrow rush out like a palpable force, threatening to sweep you off your feet. You steel yourself, pushing back against the wave of despair, and focus on the scene unfolding before you.

Through the crack you see a little boy is on his knees in the center of the dirt-floored room, his small frame shaking with sobs that pierce the heavy air. He's oblivious to your presence, his attention fixated on the imposing figure before him.

The Shadow dominates the room, its form shifting and flickering. It towers over the child, the air around it shimmering with malice.

You realize you're holding your breath. As you watch the boy, his plight tugging at your heart, his vulnerability laid bare in the face of such a monstrous entity.

- <u>Attack the Shadow.</u> (Page 136)

- <u>Sneak past the Shadow.</u> (Page 140)

- <u>Run away.</u> (Page 141)

As you descend into the musky air of the root cellar, a heavy wooden door stands before you, a barrier to the unknown, its surface marred by time. From behind it comes a soft, muffled crying—a sound so full of despair it tugs at the very fabric of your heart. Gray's tiny body trembles against your neck, his voice barely a whisper amid the oppressive silence that surrounds the door. "Are you sure you want to go in there?" he asks, his natural playfulness lost in a sea of fear. "This place gives me the creeps."

You pause, considering Gray's unease, which echoes your own apprehensions. Yet, the vulnerable cries from within ignite a resolve within you. Empathy overrides fear—you can't ignore someone in need.

The key from the kitchen slides into the lock with an almost eerie perfection, clicking into place as if it was destined to be used at this very moment. Your hand shakes as you turn it, a mix of emotions warring within you. Joy at finding the correct key is quickly doused by the terror of what lies on the other side.

You push the door open a crack, and the room's atmosphere assaults you. A wave of fear and sadness so potent it nearly drives you back. You steady yourself against the doorframe, taking a deep breath before allowing your eyes to adjust to the dimness inside.

The sight that greets you is heart-wrenching. A little boy is on his knees, his small form convulsing with sobs as he presses his face into the cold dirt floor. Opposite him, an immense

Shadow looms, its form darker than the gloom that fills the room. It is as if the creature is made of night itself, its edges blurring into the air, the ceiling too low to contain its full, menacing height.

In this frozen tableau of despair, you stand on the threshold, your next actions critical. Gray huddles close, his tiny heart beating furiously against you.

- <u>Attack the Shadow.</u> (Page 136)

- <u>Sneak past the Shadow.</u> (Page 138)

- <u>Run away.</u> (Page 142)

Descending into the root cellar, the musty air envelops you, thick with the scent of damp earth and forgotten years. Ahead, partially obscured by shadows, an ancient chest rests, its wood warped with age. It lies like a silent guardian to the deeper mystery beyond, an old, almost forgotten relic standing between you and the faint, muffled crying that seeps through the air. Gray clings to your shoulder, his tiny body trembling. "Are you sure you want to go in there?" he whispers, the usual playfulness in his voice replaced by apprehension. "This place gives me the creeps."

You pause, taking in the sight of the chest and the faint outline of a door beyond it. Gray's unease mirrors your own, yet the soft cries beyond the chest stir a sense of duty within you. Fear wrestles with empathy, but the need to help prevails.

Hesitantly, you approach the chest, the key from the bedroom held tightly in your hand. You look past the chest to the heavy wooden door at the end of the room. You can hear a faint whimpering from the other side of the door. Two locks, one key.

- ◉ <u>Try to open the chest.</u> (Page 145)
- ◉ <u>Try to open the door.</u> (Page 146)

As you make your way down the creaking wooden steps into the root cellar, a blanket of cool, heavy air wraps around you. The smell is unmistakable—the deep, earthy aroma mixed with a hint of decay, speaking of years gone by and secrets long buried. Each step feels like a descent into another time, a forgotten chapter of the house's history.

The shadows play tricks on your eyes, but there, in the dim light, the outline of an ancient chest becomes clear. Its once-fine wood is now distorted and scarred by time, the intricate carvings on its surface faded but still hinting at its past grandeur. It sits solemnly, a silent custodian of memories, its very presence adding to the mystery that permeates the air.

Gray's grip tightens on your shoulder, his small form quivering with trepidation. "Are you sure you want to go in there?" he murmurs, a note of genuine concern undercutting the playful tone you've grown accustomed to. "This place gives me the creeps." His words echo the unease that has settled in the pit of your stomach.

Taking a moment, you assess your surroundings. The chest, imposing and enigmatic, draws your attention, but it's the soft, muffled crying beyond it that pulls at your heartstrings. It's a sound of distress, of someone in need, resonating through the stillness of the cellar.

You can't ignore the cry for help, despite the apprehension that courses through you. The conflict within is palpable—fear urging you to turn back, yet a deeper, more primal part of you compelled to move forward. You steel yourself, the resolve to act pushing back the shadows of doubt.

"Don't worry so much," you tell Gray, reaching up to stroke his fur, as much for your own comfort as for his.

With a deep breath, you step forward, moving closer to the chest and the obscured door beyond. Each step feels weighted, not just by the physical descent but also by the gravity of the situation. What lies beyond the chest, behind that door, is unknown, yet the call to help is too strong to ignore. With Gray by your side, you prepare to face whatever secrets this cellar holds.

- <u>Try to open the chest.</u> (Page 143)
- <u>Try to open the door.</u> (Page 131)

The heavy air of the root cellar presses in on you as you confront the Shadow. This entity, a formless collection of darkness, stands before you in the dirt-floored chamber, its presence an icy chill against the stale, musty air. Its spectral claws, surprisingly solid against its shadowy form, loom with a threatening promise of pain.

In a burst of desperate courage, you dodge to the side, narrowly avoiding the lethal swipe of the Shadow's claws. Your heart pounds in your chest, adrenaline fueling a sense of urgency. Weaponless and exposed, you're acutely aware of your vulnerability.

Driven by instinct and a surge of bravery, you launch yourself at the Shadow, hoping to disrupt its menacing focus or perhaps create an opportunity for the child to escape. Your attack, however, is futile. The Shadow, unfazed by your desperate charge, easily evades you.

Its claws connect with a brutal force, tearing a searing line of agony across your chest. The impact sends you sprawling backward onto the dirt floor. Your vision starts to dim, the edges of your world fraying as you fight to maintain consciousness.

In those fleeting moments of clarity, you see the child, their face etched with a mix of fear and tentative hope. The Shadow, now free of your interference, redirects its ominous attention towards the child, resuming its relentless pursuit.

Collapsed on the cold, dirt floor of the cellar, a deep sense of regret and despair overwhelms you. Your attempt to protect, while brave, seems in vain. The child is still in peril, and your actions have merely delayed the inevitable. The acute pain in your chest serves as a grim reminder of your failed endeavor to confront the Shadow.

As the quiet of the cellar begins to resurface, replacing the oppressive aura left by the Shadow, you cling to the hope that your sacrifice provided the child with a fighting chance to escape. Filled with remorse for not being able to do more, you close your eyes, surrendering to the darkness. Your final thoughts surface in your head.

- <u>You're thankful you tried to help.</u> (Page 123)
- <u>You're upset you failed to save the kid.</u> (Page 40)

Hunched close to the ground, you carefully nudge the door open, just wide enough for you to slip through. The room's musty air, thick with the weight of despair and neglect, brushes against your skin as you enter. Determination courses through you, fueled by the sight of the terrified child huddled in the corner. You know you have to act, to do something, anything, to help.

Turning to Gray, you gesture urgently towards the room. "Gray, I need you to distract the Shadow," you whisper, your voice laced with tension. Gray looks at you, his eyes wide with fear, his tiny body trembling. "Are you nuts? That thing's huge!" he squeaks in protest. But as his gaze follows yours to the cowering boy, a resolve seems to form within him. With a deep, shaky breath, Gray nods, albeit reluctantly.

In a burst of sudden bravery, Gray leaps into the room, chattering loudly. The noise is jarring in the oppressive silence, echoing off the walls. The Shadow, caught off guard, recoils and lets out a haunting, mournful scream that seems to vibrate through the very air.

Seizing the moment, you move stealthily behind the Shadow, every sense heightened. The boy, wide-eyed with fear, notices your approach. You motion for him to stay quiet and follow you.

Gray, meanwhile, is a flurry of movement and noise, drawing the Shadow's ire with remarkable courage. The Shadow swipes at the air, trying to catch the nimble squirrel, but Gray is too quick, too erratic.

Reaching the boy, you whisper, "Quick, follow me, we need to get out now." His small hand grips yours, a silent trust formed in an instant. Together, you edge towards the door, your heart pounding in your chest.

But as you're about to leave, a glance back reveals a chilling scene: Gray is cornered, the Shadow looming over him, its form a swirling mass of darkness. Your heart sinks.

- <u>Wait and see what happens.</u> (Page 147)
- <u>Get the Shadow's attention.</u> (Page 149)

As you crouch down to the dirt floor and cautiously open the door, a sense of impending difficulty looms over you. The room beyond is shrouded in darkness, heavy with the scent of fear and neglect. You glimpse the small, terrified figure of a child in the corner, his body trembling in silent sobs.

As you enter, the atmosphere of the room shifts perceptibly. The air grows colder, and a sense of oppressive malevolence intensifies. In the dim light, you can barely make out the little boy crouched in the far corner, his small frame shaking with silent sobs. His eyes are wide with fear, reflecting the little light there is, and they're fixed on something behind you.

The moment you step inside, the Shadow's presence becomes overwhelmingly palpable. It's a massive, amorphous entity of darkness, shifting and swirling with malevolent intent. Despite its lack of eyes, its gaze feels piercing, directed towards you with a chilling focus.

You stand frozen for a moment, the realization dawning that the Shadow has become aware of your presence. The air around it seems to shimmer with a dark energy, and the temperature drops further, a chill that seeps into your bones. The Shadow begins to move, its form shifting and undulating like smoke, directed towards you with an intention that is unmistakably hostile.

- <u>Attack the Shadow.</u> (Page 136)
- <u>Run away.</u> (Page 141)

The oppressive air in the room claws at your nerves, overwhelming your senses. The Shadow's looming presence, a swirling mass of darkness, fills the space with an unspeakable dread. Your heart pounds in your chest, a frantic drumbeat urging you to flee. The fear becomes too much and every instinct in your body screams to escape.

With a surge of adrenaline, you whirl around, your feet stumbling in your haste. The dirt floor of the root cellar feels uneven beneath your frantic steps. Your breath comes in ragged gasps.

In your blind panic, you don't see the chest in your path. You collide with it, a sharp pain shooting through your shin as you stagger, nearly falling. The pain is intense, forcing you to limp as you continue your desperate escape. Each step is agony, but the terror spurs you onward.

You reach the staircase leading out of the root cellar and shove the door open, a flood of daylight pours into the stairwell, a stark contrast to the suffocating darkness below. The sudden brightness is disorienting.

As you step through the threshold, a chilling scream echoes from the depths of the cellar. It's a sound of pain and despair, cutting through the air and piercing straight to your soul. The scream haunts you, a reminder of the horror you've left behind, and the possible fate of the child.

◉ <u>Continue.</u> (Page 58)

As the oppressive malevolence of the room becomes unbearable, a rising tide of panic overtakes you. The Shadow's looming, sinister presence sends a deep, paralyzing fear through your very core. You can't stay; the urge to flee is overwhelming.

But as you turn to escape, Gray, clinging to your shoulder, senses your intent. "No, don't run!" he pleads, his voice tinged with disappointment and urgency. "We can't just leave him!" Gray's usual playful tone is replaced by a seriousness that underscores the gravity of the situation.

Ignoring Gray's protest, your instincts take over. You race through the root cellar, the fear of what lies behind fueling your frantic escape.

Gray continues to protest, tugging at your ear, trying to turn your head back. "We have to help! Please!" he implores, but the terror has gripped you too firmly. Your mind is clouded with the single thought of escape.

As you reach the top of the stairs and push open the door, daylight floods the stairwell, momentarily blinding you. It's a stark contrast to the suffocating darkness of the cellar. But the relief of the light is short-lived. Just as you step through, a harrowing scream pierces the air from below, echoing up the stairwell with a chilling resonance. The scream is filled with pain and despair, a haunting sound that you know will linger in your memory.

- ◉ <u>Continue.</u> (Page 58)

As you stand before the ancient chest, a sense of foreboding grows within you. The chest's ironwork is a masterpiece of intricacy, its design complex and beautiful, almost out of place with its aged, wooden frame. The lock, a robust piece of metalwork, looks deceptively new amidst the chest's weathered surface. It's a stark contrast that adds to the eerie atmosphere of the cellar.

Taking a deep breath, you insert the key, Gray's little treasure from the bedroom, into the lock. It slides in effortlessly, a perfect fit that seems almost preordained. A nervous anticipation builds within you as you turn the key. The tension in the air is palpable, and you find yourself involuntarily biting your lip, bracing for the unknown.

With a definitive click, the lock springs open. Instinctively, you leap back, your heart racing, ready for any manner of horrors to spring forth from within.

"What are you so scared of?" Gray chides, his voice a mix of amusement and anxiety from his vantage point behind your ear.

"I'm not the one shaking," you retort, though you can't deny the tremor in your own voice. "Now get ready in case something pops out of here."

With cautious hands, you lift the lid of the chest. The hinges groan in protest, a sound that echoes ominously in the confined space of the cellar. You hold the lid firmly, ensuring it doesn't slam shut, and slowly peer inside.

To your surprise, nestled at the bottom lies a beautifully ornate crossbow. The crossbow in the chest has a dark mahogany stock adorned with intricate carvings. The polished wood limbs, likely yew or ash, promise both flexibility and strength, while the lustrous, silver-like metalwork of the lock mechanism and trigger adds a contrasting beauty and ensures balance. Laying next to it is a quiver of sharply tipped, finely feathered bolts.

"I don't know why you would want that," Gray murmurs into your ear, his tone one of mild disappointment. "It's barely shiny at all."

"Do you ever think of anything else?" you ask, half-amused, half-exasperated by his one-track mind.

"Is there really anything else worth thinking of?" he replies, his question rhetorical and filled with his usual playful candor.

As you pick up the crossbow, you can't help but wonder about Gray's singular fascination with all things shiny. In a world where Shadows loom and dangers are plenty, perhaps there's some wisdom in seeking out the simpler, brighter things in life.

- <u>Investigate the door.</u> (Page 151)
- <u>Run away.</u> (Page 142)

Standing before the ancient chest, you feel a sense of unease. Its intricate ironwork is striking against weathered wood heightens the cellar's eerie vibe.

The key you found in the bedroom fits perfectly, turning smoothly with an audible click. You brace yourself, half expecting horrors to emerge.

"What are you so scared of?" Gray teases from your shoulder.

"I'm not the one shaking," you reply, trying to mask your own nervousness. "Be ready for anything."

Cautiously, you open the chest to reveal an ornate crossbow, its dark mahogany stock and intricate carvings contrasting with the silver-like metalwork.

"It's barely shiny," Gray comments, sounding slightly disappointed.

"Do you ever think of anything else?" you ask, amused yet exasperated.

"Is there really anything else worth thinking of?"

As you hold the crossbow, you ponder Gray's obsession with shiny things, wondering if there's a simpler joy to be found, even amidst lurking shadows and dangers.

- <u>Investigate the door.</u> (Page 157)

- <u>Leave the cellar.</u> (Page 142)

The heavy wooden door stands before you like a silent sentinel. The faint, muffled cries emanating from the other side send shivers down your spine. Gray's anxious voice breaks the tense silence. "Are you sure you want to go in there?" his usual buoyant tone replaced by apprehension. "This place creeps me out."

You can't help but agree with Gray's sentiment. The cellar makes your skin crawl, but the sound of fear from behind the door resonates with a distress you can't ignore. "We have to help, Gray," you whisper back, trying to sound more confident than you feel.

Taking a deep breath, you insert the key into the lock, applying extra force. The door seems unyielding. You twist harder, your muscles tensing with effort. For a moment, it feels like the door might give way, but then, to your horror, the key snaps with a sharp crack.

Stunned, you stare at the broken key in your hand. Gray lets out a soft, worried squeak. "Oh no, now what do we do?" he asks, his voice tinged with panic.

"We can't give up now, not when someone might need our help," you say, more to reassure yourself than to answer Gray's question.

- <u>Get the Shadow's attention.</u> (Page 161)

- <u>Leave the cellar.</u> (Page 142)

As the Shadow looms ominously over Gray, a sense of dread fills the air. Frantically, you whisper, urging Gray to flee, but as your eyes lock with his, you're met with a gaze filled with terror and a heartbreaking acceptance. In that brief, silent exchange, the stark reality becomes clear: Gray is cornered with no escape.

Desperation takes hold, and you try to divert the Shadow's attention, your voice escalating to screams. But the Shadow remains unfazed, its focus unwaveringly fixed on Gray. You surge forward, hoping against hope to somehow intervene, to tackle the Shadow and save your little friend.

But in those fleeting moments, time seems to slow down. Gray turns to you, his eyes conveying a depth of emotion you hadn't seen before. There's fear, yes, but also something deeper—a profound sorrow. His tiny mouth forms the words "I'm sorry," a silent apology that reverberates through your very soul. Before you can react, the Shadow's long, glistening claws strike through Gray.

As Gray's form dissolves into the darkness, he disappears as though he was never there, leaving behind a void filled with a palpable wave of agony. This intense surge of emotion—pain, fear, and despair from Gray's final moments—washes over you with a force that is physically overwhelming. It's not just the loss of Gray, but the sheer intensity of his final emotions that seem to hit you like a physical blow, knocking you off your feet.

You find yourself crashing to the ground, the emotional impact compounded by the physical jolt of the fall. It's a collision that leaves you dazed and breathless, your chest tight as if the air has been squeezed from your lungs. Lying there, disoriented and heartbroken, you're unable to do anything but stare in horror as the Shadow, now unchallenged, turns its daunting presence towards you.

The loss of Gray is more than just the absence of a friend; it's as if a part of your own spirit has been extinguished. The Shadow's advance seems almost secondary to the void left by Gray's departure, the grief and shock leaving you momentarily paralyzed on the cold, hard ground.

As the reality of Gray's disappearance sinks in, a desperate "No!" escapes your lips, your hand reaching out towards the empty space where he once was. Your body trembles as you push yourself to stand, each movement fueled by a mix of anguish and disbelief. Clenching your eyes shut, you try to shut out the harrowing scene before you, but a single tear betrays your effort, tracing a warm path down your cheek, a silent testament to the deep bond you shared with Gray.

- <u>Continue.</u> (Page 58)

In a moment of quick thinking, you grab a rock from the floor of the cellar and hurl it with all your might against the opposite wall. The rock clatters loudly, its noise echoing through the confined space. The Shadow, caught off guard by the sudden disturbance, whips around, its form momentarily distracted by the sound.

This diversion provides the crucial window of opportunity Gray needs. With agility and speed that belies his small size, he darts out of the room, his movements a blur. You waste no time following his lead, rushing to the heavy wooden door and slamming it shut with a resounding thud, sealing the Shadow inside.

Gray is panting heavily, his fur slightly ruffled from the ordeal. "Thanks," he gasps, relief evident in his voice. "I thought I was a goner in there." Despite the close call, his gratitude shines through, a small smile playing on his lips.

Outside the now-closed door, the Shadow's frustrated scream pierces the air, a sound filled with anger and defeat. It's a harrowing sound, but one that quickly fades, taking with it the oppressive, negative energy that had been emanating from the room. The air feels lighter, almost as if a heavy burden has been lifted.

In this moment, a sense of hope and triumph washes over you. Not only have you managed to save Gray from a dire fate, but you've also outsmarted the formidable Shadow. The relief is palpable, and for the first time since entering the root cellar, you feel a weight being lifted from your shoulders.

"You did great, Gray," you say, a smile breaking through your own exhaustion. "We did it. We beat the Shadow."

As you both take a moment to catch your breath, there's a newfound sense of camaraderie and accomplishment between you. The fear and danger that had loomed so large just moments ago now seem like distant memories, replaced by a sense of victory and the unbreakable bond forged through this harrowing experience.

- <u>Continue.</u> (Page 158)

In the dimly lit cellar, the heavy wooden door at the end of the room feels like a barrier to another world. The sounds of crying from the other side are muffled yet heart-wrenching, adding to the eerie stillness that envelops the space. You carefully insert the key into the large metal lock, and it fits seamlessly. As you turn it, the lock clicks with a resonance that reverberates through the room, breaking the oppressive silence.

"You ready for this?" Gray whispers from your shoulder, his voice a mix of concern and determination.

You take a deep breath, feeling the cool, musty air of the cellar fill your lungs. You look down at the key in your hand, then back at the door, steeling yourself for what lies ahead. "I don't know if *ready* is the right word," you admit, your voice steady despite the uncertainty churning inside you.

Gray shifts slightly, his small claws gripping you a bit more tightly. "I know it's scary," he says, his tone tinged with sincerity, "but I believe in us. We've come this far, haven't we?"

You can't help but feel a flicker of courage at his words. "You're right, Gray," you reply, a newfound determination creeping into your voice. "We can't back down now. That kid needs us."

Gray's presence, warm and comforting on your shoulder, bolsters your resolve. "That's the spirit!" he chirps, a hint of his usual playfulness returning. "Let's show this Shadow what we're made of."

Nodding, you turn the key, the lock clicking open. With one last glance at Gray, who nods encouragingly, you push the door open, ready to face whatever challenges lie on the other side.

Peeking through the gap, you see a young boy on his knees in the center of the room, his body wracked with sobs. The sight strikes a chord in your heart; his helplessness in the face of danger is painfully evident. He seems completely unaware of the world beyond his immediate terror.

Opposite him, the Shadow looms large, its form a swirling, flickering mass of darkness. It towers over the boy, exuding an aura of malevolence that chills you to the bone.

You glance down at the crossbow in your hand, feeling its reassuring weight. "We can't just stand here," you murmur, more to yourself than to Gray.

"Yeah, but what's the plan?" Gray's voice is tense but ready for action.

- <u>Attack the Shadow.</u> (Page 163)

- <u>Sneak past the Shadow.</u> (Page 138)

- <u>Run away.</u> (Page 142)

As you stand before the esteemed member of the Council of Dreamers, a sense of gravity settles over you. The air is thick with the weight of your decision, and the significance of this moment is not lost on you. With a deep, steadying breath, you square your shoulders, feeling the mantle of responsibility beginning to settle upon them. "I accept the honor of becoming a member of the Council of Dreamers," you declare, your voice resonating with a newfound sense of purpose and commitment.

The woman before you, a veteran Dream Weaver herself, nods with a profound sense of relief and pride. Her expression reflects not just the approval of your decision but also the acknowledgment of the journey you are about to undertake. It's a journey that promises challenges and wonders, trials, and triumphs.

As you step into this new role, you embark on a path that forever changes the course of your existence. The transition from your former life to this new realm of dreams and responsibilities is gradual but profound. Years later, as you reflect on this pivotal moment, you understand that this was when your life truly began — not as a mere participant in the world of dreams, but as a guardian and leader.

In the dream world, your role as a leader among the Dream Weavers is marked by honor and duty. You have left behind the constraints of your waking life, embracing an existence where your actions and decisions shape the realm of dreams. Here, you are more than just a presence; you are a guide, a protector, and a visionary.

Your leadership within the Council of Dreamers involves navigating the complexities of the dream world, understanding its myriad pathways, and safeguarding its delicate balance. You work alongside other Dream Weavers, each with their unique abilities and insights, to ensure that the dream world remains a sanctuary for the countless souls that visit it each night.

In this realm, time and age hold no sway over you. You exist as an eternal being, a custodian of the subconscious, forever part of a grand, ethereal tapestry. Your life in the waking world becomes a distant memory, a stepping stone to this greater purpose you have embraced.

As a leader among the Dream Weavers, you have found a fulfillment and a sense of belonging that transcends any previous experience. You have become an integral part of something far greater than yourself, a guardian of dreams and a weaver of destinies.

The End

Standing with your mentor, her offer still hanging in the air. You have always known that the essence of your happiness lies with your family – the laughter and love shared. These are the treasures of your life that no other world, no matter how magical or grand, could replace.

With a heavy heart, you meet her gaze, your eyes brimming with tears born of gratitude and a painful decision. "I am sorry, my old friend," you begin, your voice quivering with emotion. "Your offer is more generous than I deserve, but I can't leave my family. They mean everything to me. In a world without them, I could never find true happiness."

She nods, a knowing, somewhat sad smile on her face. "I feared as much," she responds. "But it's not a surprise. Your loyalty to those you love has always been your defining strength."

At that moment, Gray, ever the faithful companion, chitters softly on your shoulder, a comforting presence in this bittersweet farewell. You think of the many adventures you've shared and those yet to come, a future filled with the joy and challenges of the waking world.

With a final embrace, you bid goodbye to your mentor. As you both part ways, walking in opposite directions, there's a sense of closure and new beginnings. The path ahead is uncertain, but one thing is clear – you've made the right choice for yourself and your family.

Over the years, your role as a Dream Weaver continues to be an enriching part of your life. Your invitation to join The Council of Dreamers becomes a distant echo, fading into the background of your adventures. Occasionally, you find yourself pondering about your old mentor, wondering about the changes she feared and what became of her.

Time passes, and the talk of the Council grow silent. You often find yourself gazing at the stars, pondering the mysteries of the dream world and the waking world alike, and the intricate threads that weave them together. The question lingers in your mind – what happened to the Council, and is the change they worried about still looming on the horizon? Despite these unanswered questions, you find solace in the life you've chosen, surrounded by the love of your family and the enduring bond with Gray, your ever-loyal friend and companion in every adventure that life brings.

The End

As you near the door, its imposing structure looms larger with each step. The lock, large and seemingly impregnable, stands as a barrier to your progress. Without a key, the options seem limited. But you reach out and try the handle, more out of hope than expectation. The door remains shut.

Peering through a small window in the door, you catch a glimpse of the child inside. He's huddled on the dirt floor, his posture one of fear and defeat. The sight tugs at your heartstrings, intensifying your determination to do something, anything, to help.

"You know," Gray's voice is serious yet hints at an idea, "we might not be able to get in, but maybe we can get the Shadow to come out."

You considering Gray's suggestion. It's a risky move, but it might be your only chance. "That could work, but how do we draw it out?"

"Well," Gray continues, "Shadows are attracted to movement and noise, right? Maybe if we make enough commotion out here, it'll come to investigate."

It's a solid plan, but it's not without its dangers. "Alright, let's do it," you say with resolve. "But we have to be ready for anything once it comes out."

- <u>Get the Shadow's attention.</u> (Page 161)

- <u>Leave the cellar.</u> (Page 142)

Congratulations, you have become a Dreamweaver. You train with your mentor, the woman who inexplicably always wears a brightly colored sweater with some sort of fluffy or gentle animal on it, who is one of the toughest people you have ever met. From her you learn what it means to be a Dreamweaver.

Over the years, you grow up in two worlds, the outside world of school and houses and family, and the dream world where you along with your trusty companion Gray train and work tirelessly to save the unfortunate from their nightmares.

After many years of successful missions, most ending with the safe return of the dreamer, you are approached once again by your mentor who has been long absent from your adventures, but has not seemed to age a day despite the fact that you have grown into adulthood and begun a family of your own.

"You two have done well for yourselves in the years since we parted," she says without preamble as always.

"I had a good trainer," you nod, remembering how much she hated getting compliments. Gray, in his exuberance, runs from his perch on your shoulder and up her leg into her arms. He's never changed, affectionate as always.

"I have an offer for you, one you must consider carefully." She sets Gray down, and he runs back over to his customary place at your side. You wait for her to continue. "The Council of Dreamers would like to make you an offer. We have an open seat, and on my recommendation, they have authorized my to offer the position to you."

"What is the Council of Dreamers?" This place never ceases to surprise you.

"They are the ruling body of the Dream World and the group that monitors the Dreamweavers, typically without their knowing it." She smiles, knowing your ignorance to being monitored would annoy you. "There is a catch though, and I know it may be difficult for you to accept, but we need you, and I request, as a personal favor, that you at least consider our offer."

"There's always a catch," Gray says crossing his small arms across his chest.

"What's the catch?" You owe this woman so much for all she has done for you, you know you will take her offer seriously.

"I know you have a family in the outside world, as I once did before I joined the council. I know you love them dearly, and that your children, and indeed yourself, are still young. But to be a member of the council, you would have to leave the outside world forever. You would, as I did, stop aging and live as you are now forever."

"What if I refuse?" What she is asking is a lot.

You're not sure that you want to give up your family for eternal life.

"Before I answer, I want you to know what is at stake. There are some on the council who believe that a change is coming, that the world we have lived in and worked to protect is about to change dramatically. We are trying to stop that from happening, and we need you on the council if we are going to have any chance to save our way of life.

"I understand that I am asking a lot," she looked pleadingly at me, "but I wouldn't be asking if there was any other way."

"What if I can't leave my family?" The question holds weight with her and you see her shoulders sag in defeat.

"Then you will remain a Dreamweaver, living your life as you have since we first met. Nothing will change for you. But I cannot say what will happen if the predictions come true and out world changes. I will continue to work to save us, but this offer will not come your way again, and I'm afraid that I need an answer right now.

- ◉ <u>Accept the offer.</u> (Page 153)
- ◉ <u>Turn down the offer.</u> (Page 155)

As you and Gray brace yourselves for what's about to unfold, determination surges through you. "Ready, Gray?" you ask, feeling the familiar weight of the crossbow in your hands.

"Always am," Gray responds confidently from your shoulder. His unwavering spirit bolsters your courage.

With a deep breath, you step forward, deliberately making noise to draw the Shadow's attention away from the child. The Shadow, sensing your challenge, shifts its focus towards you, its form gliding menacingly in your direction. Its presence is chilling, a darkness that seems to absorb the very light around it.

As the Shadow approaches, you back up slowly, keeping your eyes locked on its nebulous form. Your leg brushes against the open trunk, a reminder of your recent discovery – the crossbow. The Shadow continues to advance, its form passing through the door with an eerie ease, as if the physical barrier is nonexistent.

You raise the crossbow, your hands steady despite the adrenaline coursing through your veins. As you aim, you notice a small, dark heart floating within the Shadow's chest – a vulnerable spot in its otherwise formless body.

"Now!" you shout, releasing the bolt. Gray cheers you on, "You've got this!"

The bolt flies true, piercing the dark heart. A look of shock appears on the Shadow's formless face as it begins to dissipate. As the Shadow vanishes, a wave of gratitude fills the room, a tangible sense of relief that washes over you.

The child, now free from the Shadow's influence, slowly calms down. You watch as he stretches, his form becoming less and less substantial until he fades away, returning to wherever he came from.

"You did it!" Gray exclaims, his voice filled with pride. "I knew you could!"

As you stand there, the crossbow still in hand, you feel a profound sense of accomplishment. You've faced down fear and darkness, and emerged victorious. The gratitude in the room is not just from the freed child, but from within yourself, a recognition of your own courage and strength.

The room now feels lighter, the oppressive aura of the Shadow gone. You and Gray share a moment of triumph, a bond strengthened through adversity. With the Shadow defeated and the child safe, you know that this is just one of many adventures you'll face together, each one a testament to your growing courage and determination.

- ◉ <u>Continue.</u> (Page 158)

In the dim, musty air of the root cellar, you stand with bated breath, Gray perched anxiously on your shoulder. You carefully pull back the string of the crossbow, feeling the tension beneath your fingers. Sliding a bolt into the channel, you focus all your concentration on the task at hand. "Steady now," Gray whispers, his voice barely audible. "You've got this."

With the Shadow looming near, you take a deep breath, steadying your nerves. The world seems to fall silent as you line up your shot. As you exhale slowly, you squeeze the trigger, releasing the bolt. The air vibrates with the energy of the shot, the bolt slicing through the silence.

The Shadow, sensing your presence, turns towards you. As it faces you, you're struck by the profound sadness that seems to emanate from it, a sense of longing and despair that almost makes you hesitate. "It's almost as if it wants this to end," you murmur.

Gray nods solemnly. "Sometimes, the things we fear the most are just looking for release."

The bolt strikes true, piercing the heart of the Shadow. As it does, the shadow seems to sigh, a sound filled with both relief and release, before it begins to dissipate into nothingness. The oppressive atmosphere of the cellar lifts instantly, replaced by a feeling of lightness and peace.

With the Shadow gone, you help the frightened child to his feet. He's quiet, likely still processing the trauma of his ordeal. As you lead him up the stairs, Gray jumps from your shoulder to your head, hanging upside down to look at you. "You did good," he says with a grin. "Dreamweavers aren't just about fighting; it's about understanding, too."

As you reach the top of the stairs and emerge into the sunlight, your eyes take a moment to adjust. A shadowy figure catches your attention, and you instinctively move into a defensive stance. The figure soon resolves into a woman dressed in casual clothes, her demeanor calm and reassuring. On her shoulder sits a hawk, its eyes sharp and observant.

She speaks softly to the boy, offering him comfort and promising to take him home. He thanks her, his voice reflecting his youth and the strangeness of his experience. As she leads him through a door that seems to appear from nowhere, you're left in awe.

"You have done well," the woman says to you, her voice filled with both praise and a hint of future challenges. "But you still have a lot to learn."

As you turn to Gray, he chitters with excitement. "I knew you were the right one for this," he says, snuggling next to your ear. "This is going to be fun."

"Now," the woman declares, "we begin your training." The promise of new adventures and lessons fills you with anticipation. With Gray by your side, you're ready to embrace whatever comes next in your journey as a Dreamweaver.

◉ <u>Continue.</u> (Page 158)

I hope you enjoyed your time in the dream world with DREAMWEAVER DIARIES: UNLOCKED. If you want more, join Isabella and her companion Kimi, the red fox, for their adventures in Book 1 of the Dreamweaver Diaries series

Under the Shadow's Eye

Until then, sign up for my mailing list so you don't miss the updates, and get access to the official online version of

DREAMWEAVER DIARIES UNLOCKED

~ AN ORIGINAL ~

PICK·YOUR·PATH·ADVENTURE

www.ericjohnsonwriter.com

BOOKS BY ERIC JOHNSON

Dreamweaver Diaries

Prequel: Unlocked: A Pick-Your-Path-Adventure

Book 1: Under the Shadow's Eye

Book 2: Depths of the Rebels' Stone

Book 3: Crossing Lines *(Coming Soon)*

The Second Coming

Book 1: The Lost

Poetry

The Conditions We Live

Transitions: A Story in Verse

About the Author

In a home hidden among the woods, Eric Johnson finds his muse in the quiet hours of night and the lively adventures of day.

His writing journey reflects this blend. The Dreamweaver Diaries series, with titles like *Under the Shadow's Eye* and *Depths of the Rebels' Stone*, showcases his knack for weaving fantastical tales.

His poetic side is revealed in collections such as *The Conditions We Live* and *Transitions: A Story in Verse*, published by Unsolicited Press, where words paint vivid emotional landscapes.

When he's not guiding young minds or chasing after his own children, Eric is often found climbing trees, hiking in the forest, or lost in a book. His love for coffee, dark and rich, or something a bit stronger, mirrors his passion for storytelling.

For more about Eric's work and to join a community of readers, visit ericjohnsonwriter.com. Sign up for updates on new adventures in writing and life.